JACK AND JILL

JACK AND JILL

A Love Story

Jerry Cutler

iUniverse, Inc.
New York   Bloomington

JACK AND JILL, A LOVE STORY

This is a work of fiction. All of the characters, names, incidents, organizations, and dialogue in this novel are either the products of the author's imagination or are used fictitiously.

iUniverse books may be ordered through booksellers or by contacting:

iUniverse
1663 Liberty Drive
Bloomington, IN 47403
www.iuniverse.com
1-800-Authors (1-800-288-4677)

ISBN: 978-1-4502-0219-0 (pbk)
ISBN: 978-1-4502-0221-3 (ebk)

Printed in the United States of America

iUniverse rev. date: 8/18/2010

Forward

I had decided to write the Forward to my novel when I was well into Part 1 because I forgot why I wanted to write about a heroine who was 35-45 pounds overweight—call it a condition of age. I just knew that I wanted to write a novel totally in dialogue— first person—for the reasons given below.

The personal ads at the beginning of my novel were the character outlines around which the I wrote and developed the story. I changed them to personal ads after I had completed my novel.

This is my first attempt at a novel. I have written two short stories For my personal enjoyment, both unpublished. A friend, who had read one story said that it was skimpy on dialogue. I never really thought about dialogue, I just wanted to tell a story. Then, one morning when I was exercising in the rec. room with the TV on, I was captivated by the movie Before Sunset with Ethan Hawke and Julie Delpy. I said Sue, we've got to watch this movie. It's all dialogue. I Googled it and discovered that Linklater had produced an earlier movie titled Before Sunrise. Before Sunset was the sequel. I bought both and we've watched it several times. Sue, I said, I want to write a story which is all dialogue. But about what? Which leads to my question: why a woman 35-45 pounds overweight?

Well, after my former marriage ended I kept in good physical condition with 1-1/2 hour high impact aerobic classes, weights, bike club. Don't fix me up with fatties I would request of friends. You know, just slender ones with big boobs. Typical guy thing so here I am many years later married to a wonderful, loving wife who shot from 112 pounds when we met to 60 pounds plus. For health reasons, Sue dropped it two years after I had written the forward.

I look around and see the wives of many friends who are quite heavy but absolute gems so I thought why not a love story involving a man, who views fat as irrelevant and a strong woman who likes the way she is and doesn't give a shit about losing weight and what guys think. She's happy the way she is.

If this ever goes to print or is read as an e-book and heavy woman read the forward, I can just hear their comments: "Jerry! Hello! We've been here for years. Where've you been? Glad that you finally woke up many decades later".Some guys never do. Maybe Oprah, if she reads my novel, would be concerned less with her weight and concerned more on shining and sharing her beautiful light.

No! I haven't projected myself into the novel, perhaps re-inventing myself. This guy is mature. Can't say that I was at his age. Anyway, Jack is 5'10". I'm 5'6", when I last checked. Hope that my spine hasn't shrunk more. He was an English major, I was into the sciences and the subject of English, my weakest.

There are some events which happened to me, especially the embarrassing moments that Jack related to Jill, that I've incorporated into my novel . Yes, the events happened but they're fictionalized in case my kids read my story. Others I simply invented.

About a year before I started my novel, I wrote a fun essay titled forget about the movie how to lose a guy in 10 days. Concentrate on how to live together for life in 10 days.

I realized that I could use this essay as a blueprint for their growing relationship and structured Part 1 in number of days—10— instead of chapters. At the time of writing the Forward, I had ideas on how to proceed with Part Two and have no ideas for Part 3 other than giving them a good life together.

I found that I'm close to my emotions when I write— even the short stories— in that I laugh, cry and even get aroused although I don't write explicit sex.

I hope that you enjoy my novel, whether you experience similar emotions and whether you do or don't you can send me an e-mail with your comments to: mirabella56@gmail.com

Dedication

To my dear late parents, Harry and Lena (Rabinowitz) Cutler, the gentlest of parents.

To my maternal grandparents Rabbi Shimon and Pessie Rabinowitz of Tetiev in the Ukraine.

As Stalin was intent on decimating the Ukranians, murdering marauders were predating on defenceless Jewish villages. In the village of Tetiev, 4,000 to 6,000 defenceless Jews were massacred including the entire Rabinowitz family. My mother and sister Minnie were the sole survivors of her family. Taken to an orphanage in Kiev, they remained there, don't know the number of years, until the Kiev congregation in Toronto, upon learning that they were alive, paid for their fare.

When a man's life in the village was threatened by a peasant, he escaped and emigrated to the U.S. My grandparents supported his family until he could afford his family's fare to Philadelphia where he was residing. He came to Toronto to help raise their fare.

That's where my story starts. I'm named after my grandfather: what an enormous responsibility.

Jack And Jill,
A Love Story

PART 1

TEN DAYS

SWF: About 30. Never married. Had a few short-lived relationships since graduating from college as a landscape architect. Bright and emotionally together. Well-educated, proprietor of a small successful landscape and gardening business. Own and live in an enchanted little house on a 100-acre farm. Desires a relationship with a man who has similar values and will not suffer the company of a man whose values conflict with mine. Manage my solitude creatively and will not date for the sake of dating. Prefer a male with whom I could commune with spiritually: a good sense of humour; a bit "nuts" to be interesting and fun but otherwise sensible and stable, financially and emotionally self-sufficient, kind and good-hearted. Raised by a single-parent mother, an elementary school teacher. About 5'5". Dark brown eyes, auburn hair to my shoulders—a few gray flecks— that I cut by myself. Not considered attractive and about 35-45 pounds over weight but healthy and strong from doing physical labour.

SWM: About 32, single, never married. Well educated —an English major—but prefer my career as a firefighter which gives me time to follow my passion of writing. About 5'10", lean and trim, in good physical condition. Eat intelligently and exercise regularly. Have a strong sense of self from my spiritual beliefs which I live by. Decisive! When appropriate, a great sense of humour especially when I "let go". Raised by a single-parent mother; helped financially by working after school during the school term and on construction during the summer. Was an honour student and on full scholarship throughout college.

Push, honey. Push. Bear down. Push. The head is starting to come through.

(Jill gritted her teeth, straining, eyes closed tightly, gripping the rail, Jack wiping her brow with a hand towel).

Jack, if you.. ever.....oh God!.... come near me again…

I'll...I'll Oh God!.. run the dozer... over you, gasped Jill through gritted teeth and grasping the rail tenaciously.

Push honey, it's almost through.

Here she is.... your..... lovely.... daughter. Congratulations momma and poppa. Nurse!

Quietly to the nurse: we'll probably have to do a breech extraction as per the last ultra-sound. I'll see how the little guy is positioned when I re-examine Jill.

Jack, we need to talk. The second baby will be born breech, that is feet first if I can't redirect him. It's a more risky delivery. The cord can get wrapped around his head, the shoulders could cause a problem and cause brachial plexus injuries and the like. Most of the time, the breech delivery is done via C-section if the baby is not fully engaged in the pelvic region and not too far down the birth canal. I've done many breech deliveries successfully and am willing to try the breech delivery. It will be uncomfortable and many opt for C-section.

Bottom line for me is that I want both to survive and be healthy .Let's try the breech delivery and if in your opinion C-section is required, go for it. Ok doc, proceed with the breech delivery.

Jill, I'll try to manually turn the baby while watching the ultrasound and moving him via the top of your abdomen. When I'm trying to change the position of the baby, concentrate on something to help with the pain and try not to push during each contraction. Let me know when the contractions start so that I'll stop until they stop. Jill, trying to rotate someone in your body is quite painful and I'm impressed with your courage. .....I can't turn the baby around so resume pushing.... The baby's foot is down... each contraction seems to suck her back up the birth canal..... Jill, no luck after several contractions. I'm going to wrap a piece of gauze around one foot to hold onto the baby during the contraction and to gently pull him out.

Doctor, I'm with you.....it's..... the most painful... part... Oh God!...of the delivery... for me...Oh God! ...having a doctor.... with his hand inside me... holding onto my baby's... foot and pulling him out. ...like what a vet... does when... delivering a colt.

Got him! Hallelujah! A beautiful boy, a healthy looking one too......

DAY 1

FRIDAY

Jill, I'm on my cell phone and you won't believe this. I just had a fire in my kitchen which was extinguished shortly after the fire trucks had arrived. When the Assistant Fire Chief came over to make certain that I was okay, which I was thanks to their fast response, I noticed that he had no ring on his finger. Knowing that he must be busy, I had to work quickly. He did have time for tea and home-baked cookies so he instructed the fire trucks to return to the station and started to explain fire prevention in the home. I don't remember a word he told me. He's really nice, cute, well-spoken and not seeing anyone at the moment and said yes to going on a blind date with a dear close friend—you. Although not keen on blind dates, he said he liked to keep his options open. If I had waited to call you first for permission, he probably would have been long gone.

Joan, a firefighter? I've gone out with professional men, business men, tradesmen. A firefighter? I don't know. Culturally and intellectually we're probably many light years apart.

He's nice, really cute, gentle and is well-spoken Jill. Give it a shot.

Welllll, okay. If he calls and sounds interesting, I'll see him.

✤   ✤   ✤

Hi Jill, you don't know me. My name is Jack and your friend Joan gave me your telephone number.

You're the firefighter. (Oh, I shouldn't have said that thought Jill).

Why yes! I earn my living as a firefighter. (Oh no, thought Jack, not another one. What's her next set of questions going to be: are you a professional firefighter? do you own the station?) Since we're on the topic of how we earn our living, how do you earn yours, Jill?

I'm a landscape architect, been in my business for five years. It was really tough going at first.

(Let's get it over with, thought Jack). Jill, would you like to get together for coffee, dinner, a walk? I have this Saturday off.

Sure, why not? I live on a farm. If you like, we could walk and talk. Come up Saturday say at 2:00 PM? (I'll find out pretty quickly whether there's a shred of a possibility, thought Jill. My fat ass usually turns off the typical guy).

Great! I don't have a pad and pencil with me. Please e-mail the directions to your home at firemanjack.com. By the way. How do you and Joan know each other?

Oh! She started as a client and we've remained good friends ever since.

DAY 2

SATURDAY

(Jack drove to Jill's dressed in an old pair of jeans, cotton T-shirt and hiking boots. As he drove to Jill's, Jack kept repeating to himself: don't show disappointment if she's not what you expect. Don't give her the obvious once over. She'll pick it up. Look her straight in her face, in her eyes. Open your heart to her. Determine who the person really is that resides in her body. If she's not physically attractive, will that make her an unfit, uncaring life partner, an unloving mother, bad person, friend? Of course not. Come to think of it, mother was overweight and not what you would call attractive. But she shone when you got to know her. Perhaps it's good if there's no chemistry at the outset. It could develop. Decency, integrity, joy of life, good-hearted, strength of character will outlast what western society deems as good looks. You know all this, Jack. Centre yourself).

(If he gives me the once over and stops at my ass, grimaces like most of them, it will be a short date. But, on the other hand, give him a chance. Guys are guys and they all seem to want these slim string bikini types with big boobs).

(The moment of truth arrived. Jack used the knocker—a pilliated wood pecker—and waited. Jill opened the door and they both observed each other. Jack looked directly at Jill's face which he found pleasant, welcoming and pleased what he saw. Looked into her eyes which he found to be alert, intelligent. They twinkled). Hi, I'm Jack. Jill I presume? (Jill nodded).

Jack I presume? (Jack nodded. Okay, so she's a fatty, thought Jack. So what? Are you forgetting what you told yourself on the drive up and what you wrote in your last essay… that fat wasn't relevant and meant it. Centre yourself).

(What's he thinking? thought Jill. Does he like what he sees)?

May I come in?

Of course, come in. Sorry!

Your place is absolutely enchanting. Is this all your design?

Yes. I'm an interior designer as well.

(She's a talented woman, thought Jack). You are a talented, creative woman, said Jack.

Thank you!

(Jack was impressed with the décor. Shown all rooms except her bedroom).

Let me show you around my farm. We'll go out this way. (They walk out via the back door). Why did you become a fireman? (Let me get him to talk about himself and see how long he goes on about himself).

Well, when I graduated from Honours English intending to go into the masters then doctoral programs, I needed to get a job pronto as my dear mother was diagnosed with terminal cancer and we needed money for specialized doctors and their prescribed medications. Dad was long gone. A firefighter job was advertised, I applied and was hired immediately. As well, I have a passion for writing and I knew that the job would provide me with writing time. Make no mistake about it, the training was rigorous. Mom died three years ago and I was able to take time off to be by her bedside until she passed on. I wanted nothing to be left unsaid between us. As a teen and as well as an adult, I often told her how much I loved her and how I was blessed by having her as a mother; how appreciative I was for her raising me without the help of a husband; for working those long hours so that I could receive a good education; making our home warm, happy; instilling in me and setting an example for a positive work ethic; providing our home with good music and most importantly, a love of a higher vibrational source or the creator or God whatever your belief system. Don't think me crazy, but I still talk to her. Don't know whether the message gets through but it certainly makes me feel better. But Jill, you sure are one talented woman. The way you designed your home, these mini gardens are exquisite. How'd you manage to do all that?

(Jill listened and was touched. Good-looking and no male ego. Rare!)

I too was raised by a loving single mother. Mom was originally a farm girl and wanted to expose me to gardening so she rented a one acre plot from a friend. I loved the feeling of the earth, working with earth, the land. I got permission to alter a small portion of the land with mini designs as a teen; decided to study landscape architecture at college and a minor in interior design. When mom died 10 years ago, she managed to leave me some money and with my savings put a down payment on the farm owned by the farmer, a family friend, who took back the mortgage as no bank would have advanced the funds to me. I too left nothing unsaid with mom and you're not crazy for talking to her because I do it as well. I worked for a prominent landscaping firm for five years working my butt off, learning and saving as much as I could. They were good people and understood it when I told them that I wanted to start my own business. Theirs was a family business so there was no real long-term opportunity for me. And we're still friends as well as competitors. We often refer business to each other if we are unable to do the work. They helped me get started by lending me their heavy-duty equipment and offering their counsel. With the help of my computer consultant, we adapted a computer program whereby I can show many aspects of a landscaping plan. We can show one land design then have it morph into other designs. We do the same with flowers, trees, shrubs so that my client can choose the plan they want. I cut them a computer disc which they take with them for further study and consideration.

(Talented, competent, decent. Kind of sexy. She sparks).

Jack, have you written anything lately?

Not lately. I've been working on something new that I can't discuss until I've achieved some competency—almost there. When I saw the movie How to Lose A Guy In 10 Days several years ago, I wrote an essay on it. I titled it: forget about the movie how to lose a guy in 10 days. concentrate on growing together for life in 10 days—one guy's opinion, anyway.

Do you remember any of it? Can you recite it to me, Jack?

Oh, sure! it's a personal ongoing work-in-process essay and told on several levels. I won't bore you with all levels just the basic level which I titled how to keep this guy happy.

When I drive you to work in the AM, I'd love it if you'd apply your make-up in the car and not at home—if not all the time, then some of the time—it's delightfully and excitingly feminine. I'll snatch glances of you while driving and delight in how you go about it. I'll make certain that there will always be a large clean mirror on the passenger visor. Or if we live together and work out of the house, can I watch you apply it on occasion? I'll let you watch me shave. I'll even flex my biceps if I catch you watching me. Remember: male testosterone levels are highest in the AM.

Wash and hang your panty hose and panties over the

shower bar. It's delightfully and excitingly feminine. In case you've forgotten: male testosterone levels are highest in the AM.

Make certain that you leave a huge supply of feminine hygiene products—napkins, tampons, liners and the like—in the medicine chest. A constant reminder, not that I need one but fun non-the-less, that I'm living with a woman. Leave a bit of room for my shaving brush and razor.

Don't worry about snoring. If it's too loud and I can't sleep, I'll sleep on the sofa. If you pre-decease me, I'll wish that you were back with me and your snoring wakes the neighbourhood.

Use my razor on your legs and pits. I'll love it when I scrape my whiskers with a dull blade. It means that its time to change the blade. I know that you want to be presentable to me and especially to other women. Personally, pit hair is natural and doesn't get in the way of anything. Your choice.

If you find that you've gained ten pounds or so, please consider coming to me and crying about it —I'll love it!. I'll tell you to gain 10 more pounds, that it wont make any difference to me, that there's more to grab, that women have to be fat— in the right places of course. I'll mean it!

(**BINGO!** thought Jill).

When watching a tender movie together feel free to cry—I will sort of expect you to. I invariably read the reviews in order to anticipate the emotional impact, if any, and will have a tissue or hankie ready if needed. When I'm older with less testosterone coursing through my every tissue, we could very well share some tears.

And when that time of month arrives, to a typical guy who doesn't watch the calendar, leave me a little "memento" such as maybe like a little wrapped package on perhaps the bathroom basin. In this way I can prepare myself when you can't suppress the urge to hack me to pieces with your machete. Remember that I'm reasonably sensible with a good sense of humour. Although I may lose my bearings from time to time, I am committed to our relationship. I'll realize that it's not that I've done any wrong. It's just that I happen to be there: perhaps enjoying a beer and watching a sporting event; or even at my work bench singing merrily away; reading quietly while in a state of male relaxation on the sofa with a glass of wine or even snoozing there. I realize that my simple, uncomplicated, quiet contented male self could tip the scale.

Take as long as you need to get dressed for a party. I know that a woman feels more like woman when she finally decides on the appropriate outfit reflecting the mood of the occasion; the accessories, the hair—am I omitting anything?— before going out the door. I will be nearby with a magazine and happy to offer a male's opinion—for all that it's worth— on the work-in-progress.

As well, when buying clothes, take me into the fitting room. Keeps the sales women wondering what's with the giggling.

When you first introduce me your friends say at a party or at other affairs, I feel flattered when you put your arm in mine and promenade us all over. I love being "scent-marked".

It's important for you to maintain your friendship with your girl friends—don't forsake them just because we're together. Make certain that you have your girls' night out as frequently as practical. Then I can have my boys' night out—you know them all as decent, fun-loving, caring and supportive. It's okay with me if you are still friends with a former husband, boyfriend who's a decent guy with whom things didn't quite work out. I'm the one living with you and have the confidence in our relationship in knowing that we love each other.

(Instead of being about 10 feet apart when they started

their walk, both realized that they were within one foot of each other with the occasional accidental bump into each other for which they both apologize. They were beginning to like, respect and somewhat attracted to each other).

(Jill applauded). Amazing! Do you have a sister?

No!. Why do you ask?

Oh, just curious. (This is not your typical male thinking, thought Jill. He must be gay. I have many gay friends but please God make him straight).

Jill, do you have any hobbies, interests outside of your business? I know that it's difficult especially when you've been developing your business and being a sole proprietor.

There's a group home in town housing, counseling high functioning handicapped women and I'm like a big-sister to a very loving, high- functioning feisty gal; She stays over frequently and helps me as best as she can. She's learned to bake—pies especially—prepare her meals, to count and will be able to live on her own with the aid of a part-time counselor as soon as we can locate an apartment. We go to movies and to the jamborees, occasionally to the pub—she's not allowed to drink because of medication— where we get up and dance. Beatrice loves to dance. By herself, with a partner, she's on the floor regardless. Jack, we also have girl's talk like should she be on the pill or should "I get my tubes tied"? She likes the boys and we laugh during our male bashing sessions.

(Jack was touched by this and was warming up fast. I feel like kissing her, hugging her right now. Both! Don't! Sense what's right, Jack. Don't put her off by rushing things. They decided to rest. Jill on a stump and Jack on the grass his feet stretched facing Jill).

Jack?Jill? (They started simultaneously).

You/you first—again simultaneously. (Jack gently laid his hand on Jill's shoulder, held up his hand and said you first. Jill placed her hand on Jack's shoulder). I insist.

Okay! On dates I often wonder what we'll talk about. I know that it comes with the interaction between two people if they are genuinely willing to share, to genuinely talk to each other on topics appropriate to the situation and most importantly to "hear" each other. (Jack paused, a unique thought dropped into his head). Having said that, what was your most embarrassing moment—ever?

What? said Jill surprised.

That question just popped into my head. It wasn't pre-planned.

I really can't think of one at the moment, Jack.

Okay. While you're thinking about it, I recalled this one.

My cousin and closest friend Randy and I were on a double date to our high school prom. He had his dad's new car and had already driven his date home. My date lived nearby on a farm. It was a cold cold winter evening; snowed heavily that night during the prom. The country road was ploughed and salted but her dad hadn't ploughed the driveway and it was quite a hike to up to her house. So we started to walk trudging through the snow. Randy turned the car around so that the passenger side was facing her driveway. I'm not a drinker but I had one beer too many after the prom, had disregarded minor warnings, urges, to pee and was too embarrassed to ask Randy to stop the car so that I could get out and do my business. While trudging up the driveway my bladder burst open and I peed in my trousers. Shit! Shit! Oh my God! Hot piss streaming down my cold leg into my boots I remember muttering to myself.

Why are you walking funny, Jack? she said.

Oh! It's my groin. I just re-injured it—a football injury—trudging through the snow aggravated it. Walked her to the door. Got to go, Janet, it's killing me. I'll call you. I get to the car and Randy says: hey man, why are you walking like that? How come you didn't kiss her or feel her up? She's built like a brick shithouse.

Randy, I say exasperated, flustered, soaking, I had too many beer and I pissed in my pants and I'm soaking from my crotch down to my sox. Randy panics. You can't come in and soil my dad's new car. He or mom or both will smell it and I'm grounded for the next three lifetimes. You'll have to strip before you come in. So I stripped outside the car and hung my shirt, trousers, underpants on the aerial, threw my sox away and placed my winter jacket between my butt, which I nearly froze off, and the car seat. I can only imagine what happened when Janet entered her house.

How did the evening go dear? her mother would have asked.

Okay, I guess, would be Janet's glum reply because I didn't try to kiss her or grab her boobs which she expected me to.

Janet, said her mother peering through the window: what did you do to that boy in the car or goodness knows where else?

Mother? Janet would undoubtedly have said.

Well come here and look for yourself.

They both would have looked then stared at each other, puzzled.

Mother, I swear, absolutely nothing.

Mom believed me when I got home. I heard her laughing in her bedroom. I avoided Janet until I went away to college. Oh the shame and humiliation of it all.

(Jill was in hysterics).

Okay. Mine is simpler, still laughing, and many girls' have experienced something similar. I got my first period when I didn't have a pad and it stained my white slacks. I was at a school dance. Fortunately no one noticed except my friend who saw it immediately. Went to the loo together, gave me a pad. Then we left real quick!

Wow! You were a kid at the time. You must have felt mortified.

Absolutely!

Got another one, said Jack. That one and the one I'm going to recall were defining moments in my maturation. Please don't think the worse of me for telling you this one. I was a virgin until I was 17. Not a big deal as most of the guys were despite their bragging. This naughty girl took a fancy to me and invited me to her house when her mother wasn't expected back until late. She had a reputation for breaking in virgins. A specialist you might say. So while we were going at it in her bedroom upstairs with soft romantic music setting the mood in her bedroom, her mom arrived home early with the Pastor and his wife and we were too busy getting it on to hear them. Evidently, they had just moved into the house and the Pastor asked if he and his wife cold come over and bless it. She was showing them around room for room and when they opened the door to her room all that they saw, I think, was my ass and two bodies intertwined with the appropriate sound effects. They must have closed the door quietly and tip-toed away as we heard nothing but our breathing and murmurs. When we had finished, we left her bedroom looking disheveled and were slightly disoriented. I had trouble with the zipper on my fly as I left her bedroom and she had a difficult time trying to refasten her new bra. As we entered the living room, which was on the way out, we sensed a deathly pall in the room. We looked up, me still trying to zipper my fly and she fiddling with her bra clasps, we were greeted with a stare from her mother, the Pastor and his wife that would have turned Medusa to stone. Needless to say, it was back to wanking and in retrospect a glorious interlude.

Excuse me Jack, don't look but I'm going over to the brush to pee before I pee in my pants. (Jill returned still laughing).

Are you okay to continue?

For a woman, it's hard to pee while laughing from a

squatted position in the woods, when a man that you hardly know is waiting for you with his back turned politely. Sure! Let's continue. Did you ever see that girl again?

Funny you should ask that said Jack trying to sound cute. A few months ago I was at the produce department in the local supermarket. There was this woman beside me with her husband and three young kids in tow behind her. We both grabbed for the same English cucumber, dropped it and turned to each other to sort of apologize. I noticed that she looked at me as though she remembered me, couldn't place me, then slowly started pointing her finger at me—a sort of I know you from somewhere. She was quite heavy. I then realized who she was and then I pointed my finger at her similarly. When we both recognized each other—Barb? Jack?— began laughing hysterically while hugging and swaying. Her husband, a massive hulk of a guy with fingers like cucumbers—must have been a stone-mason— looked puzzled. No! I have no idea what she told her husband.

(They continued walking, talking with the occasional bump into each other. No apologies. Just smiles).

Jack, as a fireman you must have found yourself or your colleagues in danger. Where you ever frightened?

Plenty of times but you must keep focused especially when we arrive, the flames are visible and you know that there are people and their pets inside, often pleading to be helped. It's a feeling that I can't describe and wont even try to analyze when involved in the saving of a life. I personally give thanks whenever I was able to rescue people especially babies. It's not uncommon for us, at times to simply break down and cry at the station. (Jack was about to, his voice shaky when he recalled a certain fire but recovered quickly. Jill sensed it up but wisely didn't pursue it).

What's that hut set back in that heavily treed area? inquired Jack.

That's where I go when I need to get away from the

daily pressures: when I'm sad, when I'm depressed, need time away from the madding world. To clear my mind. To meditate. It's where I usually resolve my personal issues.

Would you consider taking me there? I'd like to be there with you but, if you'd prefer not, that's okay.

Sure, come in with me.

(Jack felt the vibration immediately upon entering, sat beside Jill on the bench. Side by side, their knees touching gently. They didn't talk. Simply felt the energy, each others presence. Then simultaneously they rose slowly and hugged. Jill composed herself first and spoke).

Come with me to the drive shed taking Jack by the hand. I just had a load of green horse manure delivered in there. Got to check a few things. (Wanting and needing to test Jack's mettle, Jill walked through the manure with her work boots to the opposite side and feigned looking out the window to watch Jack's reaction in the window. Jack bent over, Jill thought, to tie his shoelace then called for her).

Hey Jill! Look at this.

(When Jill turned around, Jack underhanded a horse ball at Jill waist high. Jill stopped, shocked: hands at her side, palms forward, mouth agape, staring at the wad, then at Jack. A slow smile appeared on her face, she stooped quickly and flung a ball back at Jack. Jack smiled and they both started flinging the balls until they became hysterical, then hugged each other standing in the middle of the pile).

Hey Jack, where'd a city dude like you pick that up? still hugging but facing each other standing in the manure

Let's step outside and I'll tell you.

(Outside) One summer I was given the opportunity to work as a farm hand. After I had been there for a few weeks, one of the farmer's daughters, about my age, took me to the barnyard to explain a particular chore. She was an easy-going girl with a great sense of humour. When I wasn't looking, she smeared some manure on my cheek. Then the other kids appeared, took sides and we started having a horse ball fight. We all laughed and then got on with our chores. My job was to clean up the mess. Thereafter, nothing much ever revolted me.

(Jill wanted to test Jack for his sincerity, a test she had often used with a successful back out plan. She didn't sense that Jack was in for a one-night stand but decided to try it. Initiating a hug, she whispered in Jack's ear: would you like to stay for the night?

Jack slowly and gently released himself from the hug, held Jill by her arms about one foot away, looked into her eyes, gathered his thoughts and said: yes! and no! Yes! I'm quite attracted to you and you know it, Jill. Under other circumstances I would have gladly said yes and I've been there before. No! because I need and want to know you better, that what we feel for each other is genuine and not as a result of a turn on. You're a gem and I don't want to mess things up. I know that you're not a loose woman and you're just as much turned on to me as I to you. Intimacy will draw me closer to you and I want to know and feel that it would be reciprocated. I don't want to suppress my emotions during intimacy. If I love you I will tell that to you not only during periods of intimacy but at other times as well. Also and especially not while were both smelling and covered with manure and we don't know each other well enough to shower together. But if it's not too late, how about a cup of tea. Or if it's too late how about a juicy passionate kiss to remember you by until we next get together.

(Jill grabbed Jack by his arms, moved him to the closest wall and with her knee well-up into his crotch, planted one on Jack that he never forgot. His knees buckled. After a fast cleanup, Jack was on his way smiling as he drove home. Jill's tears were joy tears behind the door).

DAY 3

SUNDAY, REAL EARLY

(Jack dropped in on Joan to thank her for fixing him up with Jill and to make certain that she was ok after the fire).

She's a gem and I intend to see her again and again.

I haven't spoken to her Jack but I'm sure that she feels the same. (Which in women speak meant):

Joan, are you awake, I know that it's late.

That's okay. How did it go?

Oh Joan!. He's the one! He's gorgeous, funny, decent and most important, ethical. We had a fantastic day of fun. Would you believe a manure fight?

A what fight?

Yes. It happened spontaneously when I wanted to see whether he was a prissy city guy. He flung one at me then I flung one back at him and we had a real shitty, in a manner of speaking, time. Then when I tested him by asking him to stay over night, he refused saying in effect that he's attracted to me, respects me and wants to get to know me better. And soooh do I. We shared some aspects of our lives—we were raised by single-parent mothers. Joan, I'm so excited about him I hope he calls. If I were a teenager, I wouldn't budge from the phone.

Jill, knowing a little about Jack, I'm certain that he will be around tomorrow to thank me and I'll be encouraging.

Day 3, Sunday, sitting in his car parked in Joan's driveway and on his cell phone.

Hi Jill, May I come up and see you today?

I'd love it Jack. Do you mind wearing your work clothes? No, no not for that! I need help in digging a shallow trench to redirect the rain.

Then if you like, stay for dinner and we can go to the movie house in town. There's an old drama, can't recall the title, but it's supposed to be good.

I'm leaving this minute.

(Jill matched Jack with the digging, shovel for shovel then some. Jack was in shape all right but not for this type of physical labour).

Whew! said Jack at the first break. Different set of muscles.

(As the digging proceeded, the digging became easier but his palms developed calluses).

They'll be okay tomorrow assured Jill. Beatrice has prepared a delicious dinner for us. I want you to meet her. As you know, she's very dear to me.

I'd love to meet this feisty woman you've spoken so lovingly about.

Hello Beatrice. I'm happy to meet you, Jill's told me a lot of good things about you.

(Beatrice blushed and went about other business).

I hope that I didn't embarrass her.

She loved it Jack. She'll come around pretty soon.

Jill, I really have ten days off. My shift is ordinarily five days on five days off. As Assistant Chief and single, I would fill in for the sick married men and women often find myself putting in 15 to 20 days straight. I spoke to the Chief and asked him for 10 days which he gladly gave. May I come up and see you for those days?

I'd love it, Jack.

Amos, I just met a wonderful woman who lives in the country and I want and need to get to know this woman better and spend time with her. She's silk and I believe that she's the one for me. Can you spare me for an additional five days?

Jack, I thought that you'd be single for life. I hear ya son. Take it and good luck. Is she one of these skinny types that I've seen you with at our dances. You know the ones who wear string bikinis that go up and barely cover their back and front cleavages . And how they allow their pubes to be waxed gives me shivers. Love it!

Hardly, Amos. You'll meet her one day. Thanks friend.

You're cute said Beatrice coming at Jack . (Now Jack blushed).

Why thank you Beatrice. Do you say that to all the boys you meet?

Nope! Only the cute ones.

Jill intervened. Let's do the dishes later and head for the theatre. They're showing an old drama, can't recall the title but my friends tell me that it's worth viewing.

(In the drama, a cruel, brutal man is about to kick his wife out of the farm house and into the fiercest of rainstorms. Please don't she pleads. "I'll cook your meals, wash and iron your clothes, scrub the floor and do any wifely duty you desire". (At that juncture, Jack leans over to Jill and whispers jokingly and audibly enough for the benefit of those around):

"Now that's a woman who knows her place"!

(Jill smiled to herself and gently elbowed Jack in the ribs. Jack expected the elbow, feigned an oooh! holding his rib cage and smiled. The men close by, snorted and the women threw their buttered popcorn bags at him. "Pig"!)

(Jill introduced Jack to her friends in the theatre lobby).

Jill. Who's the Neanderthal that you're with? looking at

Jack who was smirking. Thought you had better sense. Just because he's cute, don't start off taking that crap.

(Jill explained/whispered. Her friend smiled and looked back and re-appraised Jack).

Jack, that there feller in the movie, joked her husband, sure made a lotta sense.(He was shot a dagger by his wife— there was probably an unresolved issue between them— and probably slept with the dogs that night and every night until he apologized appropriately).

(They took Beatrice home).

She is quite the woman, Jack observed. I remember reading how they were institutionalized many years ago by a society which neither didn't nor cared to understand them. Human beings who are capable of giving and receiving love, who can laugh and cry. Not all, but there are many who can live reasonably productive lives with a little assistance and guidance. And for the lesser functioning souls, how do we know that they can't feel, sense, experience emotions? Happiness, sadness, even experience sexual sensations. I've known some high-functioning souls who tried marriage but lost touch with them over the years. Don't know how and whether it worked for them. I knew parents of a functionally handicapped son who lived with them next door to us. We became friends when he came over when I was working on my car in the driveway. He was In his '20's and bright. His folks often told me that they hope he died before them because who would look after him? I learned of an organization that worked with what was referred to as the mentally retarded in those days and checked them out for Tom's folks. After convincing them that Tom was ideal and after they checked it for themselves, they applied. Tom was admitted into the program and flourished. After being in a group home he graduated to his own apartment which he shared with another lad in the program. When his father died a few years back, Tom took the bus to be with his mother to comfort her.

I saw him a few months ago, walking to his apartment after work:. clean-shaven, well-groomed and trousers neatly pressed. Jill, grooming is not my forte as my hair often is unkempt and when I don't shave I look like a derelict. When I saw Tom on the way home, the first thing I did when I got home was to shave.

Jack, you've got a long drive home. Why not stay over, the spare bedroom is available.

I'd love it Jill.

(They went to their respective bedrooms at about 10:00 PM. Neither slept well. About one hour later, they both an urge to go to the bathroom and arrived there simultaneously. They looked at each, laughed, then flew at each other .Jack gently moved Jill to the wall where they kissed. Jill looked at Tom, wrapped her arms around his shoulders and spoke). Do want to have another manure fight?

(Jack made the pretense of giving it a great deal of thought as he held her around the waist and said). Why don't we pretend that we just had a manure fight and we're covered with it. Do you have lots and lots of hot water?

(It was the sweetest shower they ever had. Together).

DAY 4

MONDAY

Jill, this breakfast is delicious. As I had mentioned yesterday, I've really got 10 days off and I'd like to work with you especially doing the physical labour.

I really appreciate your offer Jack and grateful. I'm pretty strong for a woman and capable of doing physical work but not like a man. Often at day's end I would leave the dishes and drop exhausted into bed. There were times when the mobile equipment which I usually borrowed from my former employers was not available and there wasn't the cash flow to purchase or even lease any. Remember your essay about forgetting to lose a guy in ten days? You only read me part one. What was part 2&3 about? Do you remember them?

I remember part 2 and part 3 partially. Do you want to hear part 2? I'll have to study part 3 but not just now. I call Part 2 the advanced level. Part 3 was the really advanced level.

Occasionally but unpredictably, give an obscene phone call to each other. Really lay into it with your choicest of word pictures. However, a word of caution: make certain that she/he is at their work station to receive the call to avoid this kind of situation: "why Jack, I never knew that you felt that way about me". "Sorry Ralph, I thought Jill was at her desk".

Every now and then have a "dirty" weekend. Call me from work and make a date. Take me to a restaurant, order a cheap bottle of wine and go to say a strip show afterwards. Tell me that if I'm a good boy/girl and behave myself, I might get lucky—I don't mean at the casino's black jack tables. Make out in the back seat? Well, if we're both are still spry, agile….

I'm entertaining a business associate at home, you bring us tea and snacks then you whisper in my ear that you want to get it on tonight even if you're not up to it. I'll try not to blush or smirk, especially when it's a female associate who'll probably figure it out.

Multi-form and manifold are the ways you can have fun with each other. You get the idea.

(They both laughed. Jill thought that there was something hopefully prophetic about parts 1&2 but let it go).

Jack, I need your help with a project that I was just awarded. Do you know how to operate a bull-dozer. If you don't I can teach you.

I certainly do! Worked with a construction company in the summers of my college years. My boss was hoping that I would work for him after graduation and taught me everything that he knew especially how to operate heavy mobile equipment.

(What more am I going to find out about him? thought Jill. Do I hold my breath, cross my fingers)? Let's drive to the construction site—the project starts tomorrow and I've rented the dozer which is on-site now. It's my biggest project to date and I really appreciate your help. They were reluctant to award the contract to me despite being the lowest bidder but decided to take a chance on me. Jack how are you at accounting, job-estimating?

I learned job-costing when I worked on construction.

I even took elective business courses at college for it: computers, accounting, taxes. We were totally computerized and integrated from the accounting to the estimating to the project management. If need be, I can buy the program and tailor it to your needs.

(Jill suppressed the urge to stop the car on the shoulder, haul him out, drag him into the woods and…)

I can do the accounting and quotations but it really drains me.

Don't worry. I was an honour math and science student in secondary school but decided that English was the direction I wanted to take along with the necessary left-brained subjects.

(Arriving at the site, they went into the construction hut). Jack, I need to make money on this project because the farmer from whom I bought the farm took back a no principal payments, interest only mortgage which matures this December 31st which is my slack season. I've managed to save about 25% of the principal owing but my concern is that my books might not be good enough for a bank or mortgage company to re-finance.

In time, Jill, I might be able to provide you with some suggestions.

Thanks, Jack. I appreciate your offer. Here are the plans. They're constructing a large outdoor mall, the largest in the area and I've been awarded the landscaping contract. Here's the disc for the approved plan that I had cut for them. I'll boot up the computer and then we can discuss the approach.

Hmm! You're very creative, Jill. Your balance of trees, bushes, plants, colours blends well with the overall appearance desired by the architect who, by the way, has created a different approach to the typical blah mall structure. Where do you suggest I start?

There's a hill at the north end that they want leveled so I

suggest that you start bull-dozing first thing. I was going to start that part next week. It'll take two few days. Okay?

Aye aye cap'n. A suggestion. To save money, why don't you lease a dump truck. After I fill it with the dozer, I'll drive it to where it's to be dumped, dump it myself, come back, fill it again until we're finished.

Jack, that's pretty ambitious. I'm not certain that you can handle it. It's quite a strenuous job despite it sounding simple and then there's always the unknown factor. And besides, it's budgeted and I can afford it.

Jill, Let me at least try tomorrow. I love physical work. We're starting ahead of schedule anyway. If it's too tiring, you can go back to the original plan.

(Jill smiled to herself. He's different from the others but non the less similar. They're united by the eternal brotherhood of testosterone).

Okay Jack, give it a shot.

(Jack, as strong and in as good condition as he was finished the project in one day instead of two and was totally exhausted. The rented truck couldn't raise its bed high enough to discharge the load completely so Jack had to shovel about 10% of each load off the bed. After a very rich dinner at a local restaurant they went right to bed. They hugged and kissed each other while in bed): Jill, I'm really falling in love with you. (He then rolled over, farted and fell exhausted into a deep sleep).

Isn't that always the way with you guys said Jill lovingly as she wrapped her arm around her exhausted man and fell asleep spoon after she opened the window and wafted away the effluvium with a towel.

DAY 5

TUESDAY

(Jack woke up well rested. Shaved, showered, dressed and went into the kitchen where Jill was in her nightie and about to start breakfast. They hugged. Jack, looking at Jill in her nightie, the testosterone shot back in full force, was about to start what he couldn't last night but decided not to. Stifle yourself, Jack).

Jack, would you like bacon, eggs, toast and coffee?

(No response)

Ahem! I said Jack, would you like bacon, eggs, toast and coffee?

Oh, sorry Jill, I had my thoughts elsewhere as he looked hungrily at Jill who picked it up—women have antennae for this. Jack, she said, there'll be a lot of time for that but we have to plan our day and you'll need your energy for— especially for —domestic jobs when we finish.

Sure! If you show me where the fry pan, skillet, eggs and bacon and all that are, I'll start breakfast if you start the coffee and toast. If that's okay with you?

Sure, said Jill pleasantly surprised.

(Jill gave Jack a tour of the kitchen cupboards and the fridge. He cooks too! Seems to be comfortable in a kitchen. I'm going to buy him an apron). Hey Jack, I thought all you bachelors ate in restaurants. You seem easy and comfortable in a strange kitchen.

I often had to prepare meals for us as mom worked long hours on two jobs. She started me on the basics when I was about eight years old and by the time I was 10 was capable of preparing a pot roast, scalloped potatoes and salad—we avoided desserts. Jill, how do you like your eggs in the morning?

Unfertilized, thanks. ..Only joking, Jack. Scrambled. You?

Soft-cooked is the healthiest but sometimes scrambled like now. That was some day, said Jack cracking the eggs into a mixing bowl and whipping them with a whisk. What a workout and we saved money by not hiring the driver. During the day I questioned the wisdom of my decision after I got my second and third winds. But boy, I feel great now! I'll follow your advice from here on. What's on for today, hon?

(Hon, thought Jill, I like that). I've leased a grader. Now don't tell me that you used to take them apart and put them back together on your lunch breaks?

How did you find out? Who'd you ask? You've had me investigated didn't you. Tricky, tricky. I did practice operating a grader after hours when the landscaping crew went home —asked the guy who ran it if he would lend me the key so that I could practice and he loaned me his spare.

This will be an easier day for you. Tomorrow, instead of having dinner here or at a restaurant, there's a pot luck dinner and jamboree at the community centre in town. We'll quit about 3:00 PM to shop and go home to prepare your dish. Got any ideas?

Not at the moment as my creative juices haven't risen to my head yet. Give me an idea as to the type of dishes that are usually brought so that I could get some idea of their collective tastes.

Usually jellied, caesar salads, rice and meatballs, store bought BBQ chicken, cole-slaw, regular salads. We don't have to get there until 7:00 PM.

That will give me time to bake a lasagna, said Jack. Do you think that would go over?

Wow! A lasagna? They'll love it, Jack.

(At the construction hut, Jill reviewed how the grading that was to be done. Jack, not having worked the grader for a few years, took a bit longer until he became adept at it. They slept together that night as they knew that they were in this for the long haul).

Jill, it might seem premature, please don't think me mad or insincere, but I'm madly in love with you.

Jack, how many times have you used that line in the past few weeks? I wanted to devour you Monday night after you fell asleep on me and farted.

I what?

Yes piggy. You did.

No!

(They fell asleep embracing each other).

DAY 6

WEDNESDAY

(On the way home after work, they stopped off at the supermarket to shop together for the potluck).

Jill! (It was her close friend Doris. Looking at Jack about 15 feet away). Where did you meet that hunk, Mmm! Mmm!

In a manner of speaking, at a fire sale joked Jill.

What?

(Jill explained).

I'm going home to tell my son to start playing with matches.

(Jack pushed the shopping cart over to them).

Jack, meet Doris. Be careful. She's single now and has her clutches ready to grab a man.

Jill, if all your friends are as attractive as Doris, then I must meet them all. Pronto!

You're such a charming bull-shitter, Jack. I'll meet you both at the jam tonight. I have a date with a decent guy that I hope works out. Wish me luck, guys.

I'm so happy for you, Doris said Jill.

(When they got home, Jack got busy baking). Jill. Where's the baking pan?

It's in the cabinet to the right of the sink. We're picking up Beatrice who's baking an apple pie.

Great!

(All three walked into the community centre. Jack with his lasagna and Beatrice with her apple pie. Doris, beaming and accompanied with a lovely looking man came over to them, wiped her brow and flashed her ring finger).

Doris! yelled Jill. We'll have a little chat tomorrow after work. Okay?

Love it!

Now introduce us to your fiancé.

Hi Jill, Jack, Beatrice. I'm Bill. Good to meet you and I hope that we'll see more of each other.

You bet! said Jack extending his had. (Jack and Bill started a conversation. Jill and Doris hugged; they would talk to each other privately ASAP).

Let's all put the food on the table, Beatrice said impatiently.

Beatrice, a young man called out, your pie smells delicious. What is it?

(Jill blushed). An apple pie.

Beatrice, whispered Jill. He likes you, do you like him. He's cute.(Beatrice blushed and nodded).

Jill!

Sally, Carol, Kate, Judy. Great to see you all. Sorry that we haven't been able to get together these last few days. I've just started a project.

Of course you have, they all said in unison. So we heard. (Looking over at Jack and giving him the once over while he was in conversation with Bill). He's gorgeous! A real hunk! We're so happy for you, Jill.

I'll introduce you to him as soon as you retract your claws. Only joking. Let's get together Friday night.

Will Jack mind giving up a night of passionate love-making?

Him? What about me? We'll both be doubly hungry when I return home.

(Mmmm they murmured in unison).

(Jack came over). Jill, I have to get something from the trunk of my car.

What is it may I ask?

You'll see. (Jack came back with a guitar).

I didn't know that you played?

A bit. Something I started about a year ago. I'll just play along with the back up band but from our table.

Let the eating begin announced the MC over the mike.

(After the meal, the tables bussed, serving containers washed and returned to their owners, the music started).

A couple got up. The wife with the guitar, her husband to sing. The wife: we'll start the evening off with a Gospel song. Ricky Skagg's Little Mountain Church.

There's a little mountain church in my thoughts of yesterday

Where friends and family gathered for the Lord

There an old fashioned preacher taught the straight and narrow way

For what few coins the congregation could afford

Dressed in all out Sunday best we sat on pews of solid oak

And I remember how our voices filled the air

How mama sounded like an angel on those high soprano notes

And when the roll is called up yonder I'll be there.

Looking back now that little mountain church house

Has become my life's corner stone

It was there in that little mountain church house

I first heard the word I've based my life upon.

At the all day Sunday singing and dinner on the ground

Many were the souls that were revived

While my brothers and my sisters who've gone on to glory land

Slept in piece in the maple grove nearby

(There followed many good amateur performers: singers, five string banjoes, dobros, mandolins, steel guitars, harmonicas and old time foot stomping fiddlers).

Jack, asked the MC from the stage. You've been noodling all night at your table with your geetar. Do you have anything to perform? Come on up.

(Jack was caught off guard then composed himself. Nodded and walked slowly up to the stage with his guitar).

Yeah, I've got one. It's a George Strait song that I heard a few years ago. Those lyrics resonated with me when I first heard it. And it still does which is the reason that I decided to learn to play the guitar. About a week ago I decided to make it into a prayer a wish a hope a dream to meet a life partner my soul-mate and sang it out to the universe. I added the lyrics of Before I Met You and it's my own arrangement.

(The women were the first to stop talking, then the men in response to them).

Anyway I hope that I will do justice to it. You're Something Special To Me. We'll keep it in "D"—Dawg—guys.

As I hold you close tonight
Hear what I say
There's no doubt it's love alright
'Cause I never felt this way
An angel's what you are
And now I see
You're not just some one else
You're something special to me
Every man, has a dream
And you made mine come true

How it happened, I don't know or care
I'm just happy I found you
(Jill's girl friends, married and single, came over to her table to sit with her, hug her, massage her back, to share her happiness that she found a loving beau. Jill had some tears).

Wrapped in the arms of love
Is where I'll be
For all the world to see
You're something special to me
It's all such a mystery
You're something special to me
I thought I'd stay single always be free
But that was before I met you
I said that no sweet thing could ever hold me
But that was before I met you
I thought I was swinging the world by the tail
I thought I could never be blue
I thought I'd been kissed and I thought I'd been loved
But that was before I met you
That was before I met you

Every man, has a dream
And you made mine come true
How it happened, I don't know or care
I'm just happy I found you

(There was a moment of silence because the audience understood what was being sung then burst into an appreciative enthusiastic applause. The girls left, Jack sat down. There was no dialogue between them. Just strong feelings. Beatrice left them alone and joined her friends at their table. They held hands, danced, exchanged loving glances until the jamboree ended).

We'll end with another Gospel. Mansion Over The Hill followed by Oh Canada.

I'm satisfied with just a cottage below
A little silver and a little gold
But in that city where the ransomed will shine
I want a gold one that's silver lined
I've got a mansion just over the hilltop
In that bright land where we'll never grow old
And some day yonder we will never more wander
But walk on streets that are purest gold
Don't think me poor or deserted or lonely
I'm not discouraged I'm heaven bound
I'm but a pilgrim in search of the city
I want a mansion, a harp and a crown
I've got a mansion just over the hilltop
In that bright land where we'll never grow old
And some day yonder we will never more wander
But walk on streets that are purest gold

So that's what you alluded to a few days ago when you said that you were developing something new, said Jill in the car as they were driving Beatrice home. Beatrice was sobbing.

I was very touched by your song. I think Beatrice was too.

Jill, do you mind if I speak to Beatrice? whispered Jack. I don't think that she's crying about the song.

Jack, maybe you're right. Go ahead, Jill whispered back.

Beatrice, you're feeling sad because you have no boyfriend that you would love to hold, kiss, hug, have sex with and have him say nice things to you?

Beatrice nodded. The crying slowly eased. But her face was still sad.

You're a grown woman Beatrice and have a grown woman's feelings.

Which means sex, affection which is normal for you, for Jill, for me and just plain anyone. Because you have a handicap you feel that any man that you meet will be handicapped as well and might not be able to tell you that he loves you or to love you like you want to be loved. That young man who called out to you. He's cute and seems okay. Do you like him?

Beatrice smiled and nodded vigorously. (She got out of the car and went around to Jack's side where the window was down).

I will promise you this, Beatrice. If you find a guy and you love each other and if he can read or sing, I'll work with him and have him sing or read to you at the jam with me on the guitar.

Promise? Beatrice said with a smile.

Promise!

If you don't Jack, said Beatrice, I'll kick you where it will hurt the most. (At that she left and scurried home).

I promise I promise yelled Jack to Beatrice's back.

Jack, you spoke to her like a loving older brother as she snuggled up to him when they pulled away. She really listened to you. I respect that.

Hon, I felt her pain and sadness and hope that I made that clear to her. I like Beatrice and expect her to be my friend as well. Is she on birth control or had a tubal ligation? You did say that you discussed these issues.

Nothing conclusive, said Jill. I'll speak to her counselor.

Hon, as well, get the name of that young man. Maybe we can play cupid. Especially if his level of competence is similar to Beatrice's.

Will do, sweetheart.

So! You enjoyed my love song to you. Why don't you tell

me about it. I'll pull off the highway and park...... over there in that ....secluded area where you can... really tell me..... all about it. Here...... in the back seat where my hearing is more acute. (Jack escorted Jill to the back seat).

Jack, where are you taking me? said Jill feigning innocence.

(They both got in—actually Jack gave Jill's butt a gentle push with the palm of his hand to indicate that there was some urgency and Jack started to get busy).

Jack, whatever are you doing?, said Jill coyly.

Can't think of an answer, honey, every last drop of my blood is concentrated in my nether regions. There's none left for my brain. A male condition.

You're a beast Jack.

I know, I know. All that education is really veneer.

(An hour later when they were still kissing and hugging, a patrolman pulled up and shined his flashlight into the moistened van window. Jack and Jill quickly covered themselves).

Jill? the officer said.

Jason?

Jack, you were great tonight. Loved your song. My wife shot me a look that said why don't you sing me a love song? Continue what you guys were....discussing. I'll radio the station that you're having a private business meeting and are not to be disturbed.

You're a horny bugger, Jack.

You're a sexy babe, I just want to keep holding onto your ass and never ever letting it go.

Kinda hard to operate a plough that way aint it ?

Naw. Shucks. Let's just digi -pic and upload it to Believe It Or Not. Maybe the Guinness Book of Records. I can read it now. Man sets world record ploughing a cornfield while holding nude wife's buttocks with one hand. The Farming

Association might want to make it an annual event at ploughing matches. Let's get the Ag. Rep's thoughts on it.

(They awoke to the sunrise in each others arms in the back seat slightly cramped. When they returned to Jill's home and when Jill was showering, Jack removed the back two seats of his van, the interior light bulb and made a note to buy a foamy mattress and bedding).

It'll be good for shopping as well. The pickup will be for everyday use. My van, for special occasions. I'm coming in now, hon. Had to finish something that needed to be done.

Jill let that one pass.

THURSDAY

Jack, do you mind if I go out with the girls Friday night? You met them last night. Sally, Carol, Kate, Judy. Doris might join us if she can get a baby-sitter on short notice. Do you mind?

Hon, It's extremely important to maintain relationships with your friends. I'd be disappointed, upset if you didn't. If you think it appropriate, tell Doris that if she can't find a baby-sitter—and Bill isn't available—to bring them over here and I'll baby sit. When I was 14, I baby sat for our next door neighbour. Only for a few months though. I learned how to change diapers then. So, if I have to again, I will gird up my loins. Otherwise, I will practice on my guitar and perhaps on another song or two.

You are a pet, said Jill, hugging Jack.

(Oooh, why do I want to leave him for even one minute? thought Jill. I hope that he'll be awake when I return. I'll make certain that he doesn't have too a strenuous a day— today and especially tomorrow).

Jack, changing the subject, trees are being delivered today by Mack's Garden Centre. We'll go over the plans at the hut as to which trees go where and how you are to plant them. How much gardening have you done?

Not much. I can learn. You show me and I'll learn.

Will do. I'll have Mack and his assistant come and the two of you can do the digging and planting. When he arrives, I'll review the process with the two of you.

(On the construction site)

Mack's truck is coming. I've got some shopping to do in town and I've arranged for Mack to drive you home. (Jill kisses Jack and drives off).

Jack? Said Mack.

Yep! That's me, Mack.

My assistant is in the truck and will be here in a minute. His name is Allan. You might notice that he's slightly challenged but make no mistake about it. He's bright and a hard worker. Allan will start you off—I've got to visit another project and will be back with lunch for us all. Hi Allan, thanks for bringing the bottles of mineralized water. Allan, meet Jack, Jill's boyfriend.

Say! I remember you. You sang that song to Jill at the jamboree. You also brought Beatrice (his face flushes and he hesitates briefly)….with you.

That's right Allan. You've got a good memory.

Yes! I do.

Great to hear that. Now you're going to show me what to do, where to plant?

Yes. Let's start digging a trench from about here to there. (And they start).

Hey Allan, slow down a bit. Let me get my juices flowing or you'll be doing most of the work.

Sorry Jack. I only know one way to work. Don't worry, you'll catch up.

(After a while, Jack did catch up and matching each other).

(During a water break). Allan, do you like music, poetry?

Allan nods. Some.

Do you like to sing?

Allan nods. I like love songs.

Good to know that Allan. Maybe you and I could do something together?

(Allan nods and they continue working).

DAY 8

FRIDAY

(Sally, Carol, Kate, Judy, Doris arrived at Jill's that night. They all wanted to get a better look at Jack before they had their girls' night out. Jack and Jill greeted them on the porch).

Hey, Jack. What are you going to do for Jill's birthday?

Birthday? When is it?

Didn't Jill tell you? It's this Saturday.

Jill?

Oh, I didn't think it important.

It is important, honey!

(He called her honey whispered Kate to the girls).

We'll go out for dinner and some entertainment. I'll have to check the local paper's entertainment page or the Internet for ideas. Then I'll surprise you.

(Their car arrived back at Jill's past midnight. They all had a few glasses of wine too many. As well, Jill's head still buzzing with advice and the type of encouragement which only close women friends of long-standing can offer. As Jill stepped out they were chanting "go girl go". Jill kicked off her right shoe, then left shoe. Left them there. Stepped up the stairs, slipped off her skirt. Left it there. "Go girl go" Opened the door and off went her slip then blouse. On the floor. "Go girl go" was faint now as they drove off. Jill stepped into the bedroom and off came the pantyhose and bra. Jack was asleep with a book laid neatly across the top sheet which came up to his waist exposing his well-defined torso, looking so peaceful, showered and innocent. Jill was about to step into the shower, took another look at Jack.

Jill looked at Jack, looked at the shower. Fuck the shower. Climbed into bed and slowly started to devour Jack who woke up slowly— appendage by each appendage).

Jill, groggily but waking fast: did you lose my place...?

SATURDAY

Oh, honey, breakfast in bed. And a long-stemmed rose as well. How thoughtful.

Twaren't much honey. Jest russelled up some of your favourite breakfast grub. You're going to be my queen for the day. Be back in a sec, as I want to bring my breakfast up here so that we could eat together and talk.

(Jack returns with his breakfast tray and both start eating).

Jack, I'm really touched that you insisted on wanting to celebrate my birthday.

I love you. Why shouldn't I want to celebrate with the universe the very day that you were born. I've planned a few things today and you're not to lift a finger unless it's to stroke me in my favourite places.

Where are your favourite places? joked Jill innocently.

Gimme a break!

The events of the day will be revealed as the day unfolds. Let's just eat and then as they say: "ladies and gentlemen, start your engines".

I'm so excited, sweetheart.

So am I honey, so am I.

(They showered and dressed).

I'll clean up and while I do, I'll straighten the mess on your desk?

A desk mess is a personal matter, dear. Please don't bother.

(Jack put the TV on for the weather). It's going to be a beauty today. Sunny in the low 80's, wind negligible and no rain said Jack.

Wonderful! said Jill.

I'm finished, sweetheart, said Jill.

So am I.

First on the agenda is to walk the sacred earth. We did to some degree on our first day. A care-free walk without having to think of work. (Jack took of his shirt to catch the sun. Jill gave him the once over and felt warm, gaga. Her eyes showed it. They came to Jill's secluded area and hut).

Jill, honey, may I enter?

Jack, that's for when I'm depressed. My private sanctum.

I know, honey, but please let's go in. I'll explain shortly.

(When they entered and lit the lamp, Jill jaws dropped. There was a foam mattress with new bedding, twelve long-stemmed roses and a bottle of Jill's favourite wine chilling in a portable cooler).

This will be our honeymoon suite for life. For every time that you came in here and feeling depressed, we'll counter it with something to celebrate.

I don't know what to make of this, Jack.

Jill dearest. The last thing that I want to do is to desecrate your sacred site. What I meant by all this is now that we're in each other's lives, that we have each other; that we can help each other in times of personal difficulty, sadness, depression; to share our joys as well. There will be times when you need and want to be alone, I'll understand and respect that. You or I or both of us could possibly resolve these problems, be they personal or business, in this sacred site. (Pauses for three seconds). Maybe this wasn't such a good idea Jill.

Jack, you dear man. Sit down here beside me and open the wine.

(Jack opens the wine, pours it into two plastic cups).

I was taken aback by all this upon first view. My head hadn't made the connection that you, dearest, are in my life and I do want to share everything with you. This is now our sacred site.

It's strange but I am picking up the vibration of your sadnesses of times past. It wants me to go back to be there with you. Not to resolve your issues. No one can but you. Overcoming these issues is a personal growth victory. I simply wanted to be there with you sending energy, love, support.

(Now Jill's hands started to get busy and they were in each others embraces until they slept it off until mid-noon). They both awoke together having to relieve themselves).

Oh, I almost forgot, said Jack. There's toilet paper hidden back there in a zippered case along with a his and hers water spray bottle.

Calculating scheming beast, joked Jill. Love it!

You haven't seen the half of it, said Jack, gathering up the bed sheets and carrying them back to the house along with the sealed bucket.

(As they were walking back). Jill, you know that we both love country, Appalachian, blue grass, hillbilly and the like. Well, over in nearby Mule Kick they have the Redneck Revue which has dinner and a show. Their web-site said that they have a troupe of international entertainers so I made reservations.

Jack, that's a wild town and 60 miles away. I haven't been there in years. Sounds exciting, let's go.

(They enter the house and Jack drops the sheets into the

laundry hamper in the bedroom. They both undress and shower together).

Let's get cracking or we'll not get there on time. From what I read of this place, a sport jacket and tie are required. I Googled a scenic route and we can take our time driving there. We'll take my van. Our dinner reservations are for 7:00 PM and the show doesn't start until 9:00PM.

(Jack open's the door for Jill).

Jack, there's no interior light.

Damn!

Jill momentarily caught sight of the back of the van as she was entering—the foam mattress and some cut flowers. Giggled to herself and settled in.

(Arriving at the Redneck Review). Jill, if you don't mind, wait at the door while I park the car.

(Jack returns. On the lawn are old rusted beat up pickups, some on blocks looking as though they were being worked on; open refrigerators, beer bottles were strewn all over).

Jack, this must be some joke. I feel like throwing up. Look at the chalk board with today's special. Braised squirrel in a creamy chestnut sauce? garnished with boiled turnip and corn breaded possum tail? Soup—boiled crawdads and roasted geckos? Dessert. Sweet and sour toad? Coffee with a dollop of "shine"?

I wanted to surprise you with regional foods. I'm certain that you'll love it. They've removed the fur from the little critter and there's a cherry tomato in its mouth.

Jack. No!

Hon, Jack whispered. It's all tofu. Shaped like squirrels, toads, crawdads and geckos. The chestnut sauce is for real and I hear it's delicious.

Jill giggled. Jack, you're impossible. Let's go in. I'm starved. Even for tofuded squirrel. (Takes his arm).

(They are greeted by a toothless maitre 'd wearing coveralls).

We have a reservation for two at 7:00PM.

Jack and Jill? Yep! Y'all just follow me. (Leads them to a front table where Jack pulls out Jill's chair and seats her).

Whuch y'all have to drink, asked Suzy Mae their server?

Hon, would you like a carafe of their house wine?

I'd love it.

A carafe of your house wine, Suzy Mae please.

Comin' up, honey.

Jack, this place is really jumping. I think that I see some familiar faces here.

Do you want to go and introduce ourselves or wait until they do?, asked Jack

What's your preference, dear.

A quiet dinner, hon. Just the two of us.

Here's your drink, honey. Suzy Mae was fast on her feet.

Whuch y'all havin' for dinner.

Jack looked at Jill who nodded.

Suzy Mae, we'll have two of your special. Hon, how do you like your squirrel—rare, medium, well done? joked Jack.

Honey, we only have it done one way, smiled Suzy Mae.

Okay.

Jack, this I've got to see. Braised squirrel?

Jack poured the wine into their glasses. Jill, these past nine days have been the happiest in my life. I'm nuts about you. I love being with you, working with you, sharing your home with you; me touching you, you touching me, our intimacy, preparing meals together. Every cell resonates when I'm with you. You're the angel that I prayed for in that song that I sang to the universe. I'm in love with you. Madly!

Jack dearest. I'm touched by that.

They both sipped their wine.

Jack, I gave up hope of ever finding a man that I could truly love. You're fun to be with, sincere, ethical, good-natured, intelligent, sensitive, no ego and I love your body as well.

Shall we leave now to consummate our appreciation of each other? It's mighty tempting. You don't want to take home braised squirrel in a doggy bag do you?

(Suzy Mae brought the dinner).

Y'all enjoy your dinner, you hear as she placed the platter in front of Jack and Jill.

Jill eyed her plate for a few minutes. (There was an understandable reluctance).

C'mon hon, dig in said Jack chomping away purposefully with an uncharacteristic full mouth of food, it's delicious.

Jill took a deep breath, cut a small piece from the squirrel's thigh and placed it slowly in her mouth, her eyes closed. Began chewing slowly. Stopped. Her eyes popped open. She smiled. This is absolutely delicious!

Is your squirrel male or female, hon? I know that the chef is a stickler for detail. Look under the tail and if I remember my zoology there should be two little wee things there. I'll check mine.

Well lookee here, said Jill. Can you imagine? Here, let me pass you one in my dessert spoon. I hear that if you eat enough of these you'll be jumping from tree to tree looking for and burying, if you pardon me, your nuts.

As long as I know where they are, smiled Jack.

If y'all finished I'll take your plates, said Suzy Mae. D' y'all want your soup?

Sure nuff honey, replied Jack.

Jack emptied the remaining wine into their glasses.

Here y'alls' soup as Suzy Mae served the boiled crawdads and roasted geckos in steaming hot bowls.

Jack! This is absolutely delicious. We'll have to read up on tofu for our meals.

Anything and everything in moderation, hon.

(They finished the soup, had the dessert and coffee with the dollop of "shine" which was really Irish Whiskey. They both started their coffee with a sip and quickly sat bolt upright).

Jack dearest, said Jill coyly, you don't have to get me stone drunk to bed me. I'll be soooo unresponsive. Like you'll be making love to a warmed over corpse.

Whew that's strong coffee. That's not a dollop of Irish Whiskey. It's a wallop.

The sweet and sour toad was absolutely delicious. The chef is a genius. I don't think I'll prepare the dishes that he made—faux yuck—but I'll certainly try the tofu.

Great, we'll work together in the kitchen.

I'd love that, Jack.

May I bus y'alls' table? as the show is about to start, asked Suzy Mae.

Sure nuff, honey, said Jack.

(Just as the MC was about to announce the evening's entertainment Sally, Carol, Kate, Judy walked in and sat at a nearby table).

Hey girls, come over to our table and join us. Here, let's move this table over.

(Jill didn't see Jack put his finger to his mouth).

Ladies and gentlemen. You're in for a gen-you-ine international evening of terpsichorean artistry. And now, ladies and gentlemen, from the Holy land, Israel. Put your hands together forrrrrr: Gedalia and His Kosher Genitalia.

The curtain parted and out came Gedalia sporting a beard, side curls and the traditional garb of a medieval Jewish berger. The band started with a slow sexy Hatikvah and Gedalia, between genuflecting and clever choreography, stripped down to his jock which had a Star of David prominently placed. Did an Arabesque, which got the women's attention, especially the zone with the Star of David, worked it into a Pirouette, then a bump a grind, wrapped himself in a prayer shawl and sashayed off the stage kissing a mezuzah which was on a post at stage right. There were Jewish college kids in the crowd who were going wild including Jill and the girls. The house was going wild. Gedalia was a great opener and knew how to work an audience. Jack found it amusing and downed his first beer.

How was Gedalia? asked the MC. The audience clapped and yelled. Makes you want to do something Jewish like going to a Chinese restaurant. And now, ladies and gents, from Hong Kong—the curtain parted—let's have a hand for...... Wong and His Hot and Sour Shlong. Wong came out traditional Chinese peasant attire. The band started with a slow Chinatown my Chinatown. Wong slowly removed all down to his jock displaying a magnificent dancer's physique, whirled and twirled, pretending to dip his jock first into a soy sauce cruet then into a plum sauce cruet. Jill nearly choked on her cocktail. The girls were yelling, clapping including Jill after she composed herself. Kate slipped him a five dollar bill wrapped in a piece of paper with her telephone number which he stuffed into his jock. Kate clapped her hands and was in hysterics. As were all the girls. Jack downed another beer.

Hey girls, maybe Wong will be your server at the Chinese restaurant yelled the MC.

We wish, we wish cried out the women.

Jack finished his beer and ordered another. The beers helped him to loosen up and he was smiling, laughing during the performances.

Jack, you sneak. You knew all the time.

Yep!

This is hilarious. These guys were great. Real showmen. Jack, please be careful as to the number of beer you are drinking as you rarely drink and that you have a low tolerance for alcohol. Wine then the spiked coffee?

Hon, I can't believe the show. It's hilarious. This is a very very special occasion and if neither of us can't drive, I've made other arrangements.

Like what?

It's a surprise.

Okay!

And now from Scotland. Folks, this is the most unique dance act ever to appear on North America stage and you will be the privileged few to say that you saw it first. Here. In the Redneck Review.

(The curtain opened and a Scottish piper walked out leading a handsome man wearing kilts and supporting a rooster on his forearm).

Let's hear it for……. Jock and his cock.

Jack nearly choked on his beer. Jill and the girls were on the floor.

The piper started with the traditional Cock O' the North at a slow tempo, Jock whirled and danced with the rooster, which remained calm, then settled it on a roost and began his gyrations.

Oh no Jock, not anotherrr Scotch bestiality act, yelled an inebriated patron. Another yelled: Hey Jock, wherrre arrr yerr trrrooosers?

Off came the sporran, then the kilt, tossed his tam off to the side. The rooster was calm and occasionally fluttered his feathers on his roost.

Hey Jock, yelled a drunk patron, yerrrr not supposed to wear anything underrr yerr kilt, laddie. Especially a jock, Jock.

(By now Jack had long exceeded his capacity for beer and was cheering along with the girls).

That's the show for tonight folks. Wait a minute. Gedalia whispered something to Jock who handed him the rooster.

Gedalia placed a yarmulke on his head, waved the rooster over his head, started genuflecting and seemingly was mouthing a prayer.

Hey! yelled one of the Jewish college kids, he's saying Kapporet and they went hysterical. Gedalia stopped when he felt that he milked the situation, returned the rooster to Jock, blew a kiss to the audience.

Now that was sumthin' said the MC. Hey folks! One act from the Ozarks didn't show —Yokum and His Red-Neck Scrotum. We have some time left. Anyone in the crowd have the guts to come up and strut their stuff? looking around at every male in the crowd.

Jack, with his inhibitions totally stripped away said yo!, I'll try.

Jack, sweetheart, are you nuts?

Where you at? asked the MC.

Yo, over here, waving his hand.

Ah hon, it's all in good fun, slurred Jack.

Hey folks, now here's a brave man. Give him a hand. What your name sonny?

Just call me Jack.

Whuch you gonna dance to?

Jack thought, reeled a bit— how about David Rose's The Stripper.

(Jill placed her hands over her face, hysterical. The girls were interested, curious as to Jack's attributes).

(The music started and Jack started to bump and grind. Off came his tie—flung it . Then his shirt, his belt, trousers all flung casually here and there, leaving him in his jockey shorts, loafers and sox, removing the latter in a sensual manner while seated on a stool, then sashayed: bump, grind, over to the girls' table and placed his crotch on the corner of the table where Jill was sitting with the girls who were drinking Jack in reeaaal good. Jill gestured with her fist as though she was going to smash his jewels—while hysterical.

Jack whirled away, bump, grind and the music stopped. Jack bowed and gathered his clothes, changed in the restroom and rejoined the girls).

Whew, that was difficult trying to improvise. I know that I had a few beers too many but this wasn't planned. Did it look okay? I think that I stumbled a few times.

You did fine said the girls in unison.

Your drooling is too obvious and stop undressing him Jill whispered to them. Get your own men.

(They all left together and walked to Jack's car to say goodnight. When Jill was escorted in they saw the mattress and flowers and began to giggle).

What's so funny? asked Jack.

Oh!, said Carol. Your act was hilarious.

Really?

The girls left giggling.

Jack shook his head. Hon, there's something that I've to show you in the back seat.

Oh, pray tell what? asked Jill innocently.

(As Jack helped her into the back and onto the mattress with a glad hand he presented Jill with the cut flowers). My Queen for the best day of my life and I'm going to seduce you. As he started to get busy—I've got to throw up. The bucket, fast.

I suppose you've got wet napkins somewhere here? asked Jill when it seemed that Jack was finished.

(Jack simply pointed to a corner).

Sit back here sweetheart, I'll drive us home.

Jill, I love you then closed his eyes while Jill drove home.

DAY 10

SUNDAY

(Jill awoke early. Jack was still sleeping it off).

Where do I stand with Jack? thought Jill. This is his final day. The 10th day. They've passed so very beautifully and we really haven't discussed what's next. I know Jack has been working hard. Seems to enjoy it and has told me many times that he loves me and I believe him. I love him so much that it hurts. This has been the best 10 days of my life. Jill, take hold of yourself. Jack's the most decent, honest man you've ever met. Broach it with him gently when he wakes up.

Wake up wake up, Jill was shaking Jack vigorously.

What, what's going on? said Jack groggily.

Jack, your vacation ends today and you haven't discussed your intentions with me, us.

Oh yes, said Jack as he rolled onto his back and slowly sat up propping up his back with his pillow. Took a minute to clear his thoughts, placed his hand over his eyes in preparation to say something difficult and said: Jill, I've been doing a lot of thinking. It's been a lot of fun and it's difficult for me to have to tell you this—Jill started to feel sick to her stomach, then livid, she's been had, lied to in the worst way a woman could be lied to———— I quit my job and want to be with you for the remainder of my life.

You bastard, said Jill swatting him in the shoulder.

Ohh!!! Said Jack holding his hand on his shoulder pretending that it was broken.

Amos, I love this woman and want to be with her for the rest of my life and don't want to return. Forget my vacation, holiday pay and any unused pay credits. Please don't ask me to give you adequate notice as that will mean weeks without Jill. She can't leave her business as she's just begun a huge project and I'm helping her.

You know Jack, you made me a lot of money. Everyone was betting that you'd be back on the job in ten days. I bet that you wouldn't. Been grooming your successor these past days. You know Dianne and her husband. She's, a bright, talented and dedicated woman .I'll arrange everything on two conditions: (1) When you've learned to keep your hands off each other for at least three hours, you are to bring Jill to our place for dinner. Sophie is anxious to meet her. (2) Both of you are to show up at the Christmas dinner. They all want to meet you and Jill. Those are your orders. Best of luck to you and Jill, son. I'll take care of your resignation.

What's more, and with or without your approval, I've put my house up for sale. It's still a seller's market in my part of the city. Don't know how long it will last and I don't want to speculate in real estate. I'll take my profit now. When the sale is finalized, I'll allocate enough money to discharge the mortgage when it's due—December 31st you said. If it's not sold by December 31st, I'll arrange bridge financing, secured by my house to discharge the mortgage. As well, I'll buy a T-Bill in order to secure a line of credit at favourable interest rates so that you'll be able to operate much more efficiently. But let's understand one basic fact. Jill, honey, this is your business. You still will call all the shots. I'll help where I can with the physical work as I've been doing and to learn the business as best as I can. I will also do, if you say so, the admin work—the accounting, taxes and my share of household responsibilities. We can do the job quotes together. I hope that you're not angry with me for not sharing this with you all along. I'm not a closed, secretive, unsharing person. I knew by the end of day four that I wanted to spend the remainder of my life with you and wanted to surprise you. Remember when we were standing in the manure and I refused your kind offer to spend the night with you? I wanted to be certain that you would feel for me as I would feel for you. I sensed that when we took our first shower and slept together but was totally convinced by day 4.

With tears in her eyes: don't get out of bed, you wonderful, delightful, bastard man of mine.

END OF PART 1

PART 2

WEDDING PLANS
(A few weeks later).

CHAPTER 1

(While lying in bed). Jill hon, when my house is sold, I'll donate my meager furnishings to charity. I bought most of it in garage sales and thrift stores. The only possessions that I'll bring will be my laptop, books that I treasure—not too many—toothbrush, shaving brush and razor. I'll have to check whether the medicine chest has room for my brush and razor.

Oh, I'm certain that we'll make room said Jill with a smile remembering part 1 of Jack's essay on 10 days.

Would you like to open a joint bank account for household expenditure? asked Jack.

I'd love it! Jack dearest, remember the essay you wrote about forgetting the movie how to lose a guy in 10 days and to concentrate for 10 days on how to stay together for life?

Yes. Of course, honey.

Do you think it was prophetic? That we met and then fell in love—in 10 days!

I never thought of it said Jack genuinely. But, come to think of it, we were living that script. Prophetic? Perhaps. I prayed to the universe for a soul mate and you came into my life.

You never read the third part to me.

That's correct because I couldn't remember it in its entirety and I promised you, myself, to memorize it which I did. I called it The Really Advanced Level. I wrote it for myself, a guide so to speak, so that when I met the woman I wanted to spend my life with we would both build on it to develop the foundation for a solid workable marriage. Observing some couples, I've heard cutting sarcasm, harsh criticism, hurtful name calling all of which inflict profound and enduring harm in their relationships. I resolved, promised myself not to let this infect my relationship with my wife.

I'd love to hear it. Will you recite it to me?

I'd love to. Let me take a loo break and then I'll be ready.

Don't flush, I gotta go too.

(They both sat up in bed with their pillows at their backs against the headboard).

If you are angry with me, make a personal statement. i.e. "Your remark about the subject really upset me" . No name calling—"you're an idiot. No insults—"do you have shit for brains"? No generalizations—"you're always doing the same stupid thing".

Don't react to something I've done but respond. The latter, to me anyway, means that you've given consideration to your thoughts, actions, comments. My dear mother always cautioned me when I was a kid: "as long as it's in your mouth, you own it". To this I add: before you say or do anything to anyone, decide on the relationship you want to create.

When possible, resolve a heated issue that same day. Don't leave issues unresolved because they'll fester and worsen. Both of us will sleep better after resolving a personal issue. Makes cuddling even sweeter.

If I don't understand what you've just said to me based on my response —I might be in my own thoughts which I often am and my privilege—don't fly off the handle. Tell me that you don't think that I really heard you or if I did hear you, repeat it, paraphrase it back. Any misunderstandings should be rectified at that time.

If it's obvious that I'm busy with something or another, on a long-distance telephone call, don't barge in on me. Ask me, signal me or lip-speak it—how much time, when can we talk? I'll realize that you want to talk and signal an estimated time with my fingers/hands. If it's an emergency, get my attention immediately, in any way.

Don't "mind fuck" me. Don't tell me how I'm to think about a given subject. No one has any business in another person's mind. You're there by invitation only.

It's wonderful if we both share the same values and are of one accord spiritually.

It's very basic but a workable guide. What are your thoughts about this being a blueprint for us? We can build on this as we live our lives together.

Jack dearest. That's a wonderful device for loving communication. We should review our day every evening before going to bed just in case there is an issue that needs resolution that we perhaps suppressed, overlooked during the business of the day. If something needs rectification, reconciliation either between us or others, we should address the issue or issues. If the day went well, then hugging before rolling over would be especially sweet. Nothing must prevent us from hugging each other at bed time. We don't have to make love every night but we should at least hug and be affectionate with each other.

Yes, hon. In the morning and instead of jumping out of bed and rushing about, let's focus on what needs to be done and how to approach it in a fair and ethical manner. Let's make a good life together. Let's get married say mid- December, yours, whoops, our slow season. No living together, not that I'm against it, but I want a deeper commitment for us. How do you feel about it?

Make love to me dearest and I'll give you my answer.

Hon, give a guy five minutes.

CHAPTER 2

Jill, honey, my cousin Randy, with whom I've been close since time began for me, will be my best man. We're about the same age.

Randy, I've met this wonderful woman whom I believe is my soul mate, the one I'll marry. I've arranged 10 days off to work with her in her landscaping business.

Have you two been intimate?

No, but that's not an important issue to us right now. Any fool can have sex. We want to get to know each other better... that we like and respect each other..,, that our values our thinking are compatible.

What's she like?.

You know Randy, all my dating life I was attracted to these slender babes with big boobs—you know, typical guy stuff. That we'd hike and bike together after a long bike-ride or hike, fuck somewhere in a wooded patch off the main road with the sun shining on my ass through a clearing in the canopy. Jill's in her ealy thirties and about 35+ delightful pounds overweight.

Oh, then she and Audrey will hit it off.

Knowing Audrey and Jill, they'll hit it off regardless of weight. Women have this uncanny ability to sniff each other out instantaneously as to whether they'll relate to each other and how. Pleasant face, eyes that are alert and twinkle, auburn hair to her shoulders, when not working otherwise a bun; very bright, accomplished ,perceptive, open and honest with her thoughts, sincere and communicative, fun to be with, earthy, a hard worker. Is an extremely creative landscape architect and interior designer.

Jack, Audrey and I will send you and Jill good energy and hope that it will work out. Hey, if it does, can you imagine little cousins, close in age surrounded by two person families—a rarity in these times.

Give Audrey my love, she's the best thing that's been thrown your way. I'll speak to you in a little over 10 days.

Jill hon, have you given any thought as to a maid or matron of honour?

(Jill thought for a few seconds). I'd like Beatrice.

Beatrice? Hmm! Jill hon, she'll be touched. Honoured!

I'd like to make it a small wedding inviting those who've been close to me over the years—my guys and gals at the fire hall and their spouses—about 16 with spouses, dates. Whenever the station had a party we'd potluck it and the food was always prepared with love and care. Would you mind a pot luck wedding? Hey! I almost forgot my closest friend, my cousin Randy and his wife Audrey. I know that I haven't mentioned them since we met. No! Actually once in that embarrassing moment story. What are your thoughts, hon?

I feel the same way, dearest. In our part of the country, we're neither rich nor are we pretentious. We can rent a large tent, heaters, table, chairs and table cloths. It usually doesn't snow in mid-December or if it does, it doesn't last.

CHAPTER 3

(Jack on speaker phone with Jill sitting beside him). Hey Randy, how are things? I'd like to…about to introduce Jill)

(Randy jumping in). Have you fucked her yet?

(Jack placed his head between his hands, dropped it and began to chuckle).

Hi Randy, this is Jill on our speaker phone. (Giggling).

And this is Audrey on our speaker phone (who clapped her hands in laughter).

Yes many times Randy and it's been absolutely fabulous. I'm sure that Jack will fill you in when you have your boy's night out.

Oh shit! Jill, I'm terribly sorry if I offended you with our guy talk.

Jill this is Audrey and I'm really looking forward to meeting you. If you want to see intense red embarrassment— more like crimson— it's on Randy's face.

Audrey, I would love to meet you and Randy. Oh Randy, don't worry. I don't offend easily with guy talk. Women find most of it amusing, predictable. Bye now, we'll meet soon and give Audrey my love and can't wait until we meet. I know from Jack that you're a really sweet decent guy. Here's Jack.

Okay Randy, the speaker phone is off.

Jack, she's sounds like one terrific gal. How did you meet? (now less crimson).

You know Randy, there are times when you ask, beg, pray to the universe, you sometimes get an immediate response.

What do you mean?

I was so disenchanted, discouraged, depressed over my social life that one evening I sang, asked, prayed if you will, a George Strait love song to the universe asking, praying to meet my soul mate. The next day we answered a small residential fire alarm which we extinguished. The woman, Joan, was delightful and asked if I'd join her for tea and home baked cookies. I discussed fire protection in the home. She then asked if I go on blind dates as she had a lovely friend—Jill. I said fine, although skeptical. I called Jill just before my five days off. I drove up to her farm praying to myself to open myself to her, not to be hung up on looks. When you visually undress the women that I've been going with, they all started looking alike.

Shit, Jack. I don't think that I could have passed that test when I was single.

You would have Randy. The moment of truth arrived. I knocked at her door. She opened the door and there she was: smiling, welcoming me. I looked directly at her and saw pleasantness, a twinkle in her eyes, she was alive man! We talked and walked her property—she has 100 acres most of which are beautifully cultivated. As we walked and talked we shared parts of each others lives. She too was raised by a single mom. The more we talked and listened to each other the closer we were drawing to each other. So close in fact that we had a horse manure fight.

You had a what?

You heard me right. But I'm not going to go into it in detail until we get together. Hold the line for a minute. (Whispering). Jill hon, I like to invite Randy and Audrey for dinner two Saturdays from now. How do you feel about it?

That's fine, dearest.

Audrey, Randy, Jill and I would love to have you over

for dinner not this Saturday but the following Saturday. Can you make it mid-afternoon so that we can show you around the farm then come back and be relaxed for dinner and not rushed?

Can we! Hang on for a minute.

(Whispering). Audrey, we've been invited to dinner at Jack's and Jill's place the following Saturday. Okay?

Absolutely! How wonderful! I can't wait to meet Jill and to see your hunk of a cousin whom we haven't seen in weeks.

Jack! We're on!

Great, I'll e-mail the time and directions to our place. I forgot. Does Audrey have any food allergies? E-mail me us if she does.

And now to call Amos and Sophie.

Hello Amos, Jack and Jill here.

Hi kids how are you? Both of you have been in our thoughts.

Are you and Sophie seated?

Oh oh, what's up?

Tell me something, Amos, are you still a lay minister and a J.P.?

Yes, why do you ask? Do you need some type of affidavit certified?

Jill and I have decided to get married and there is no one else that I want to marry us, Amos. You've been like a father to me all these years.

Jack, son, it would be my pleasure. Now here's Sophie, she wants to speak to Jill.

Jill dear, I can't contain my tears as I am so happy for you and Jack. He's been like a son to us and I'm so very anxious to meet you.

Sophie, Jack and I would like to have you and Amos over for dinner on the third Saturday. Is that okay?

It most certainly is, Jill dear.

That's wonderful Sophie, Jack will e-mail directions to our home. Oh! Do you and Amos have any food allergies?

Thank you for asking, Jill dear. Yes! We both avoid dairy, wheat and sugar.

Then there shall be none.

(Call ended).

Amos, how considerate they are to ask us about our food allergies. No one seems to ask nowadays.

Jill hon, let's chart the steps to our wedding. We have about five months to go. I have a planning calendar and we'll start charting now. Randy and Audrey for dinner two Saturdays from today. I'm to e-mail them directions and whether any food allergies. Sophie and Amos three Saturdays: wheat, dairy, sugar allergies. What about your friends? Hey, the girls? Beatrice?

Why not have them over on the fourth Saturday?

Let me call them and see what their plans are. I feel that they might want to take me out and work me over like: hey girl, this is your last night before you lose your freedom and enter into a life of diaper drudgery. Let's all cut loose.

Shall I start buying you frumpy drudgery clothes now? Actually honey, I insist that you always have your night or nights out with your girl friends. You'll need it. It's healthy and they're fun. If I feel that my ears are burning I'll know that I'm one of the males being bashed. And I promise never ever to ask what you guys discussed. I usually had my nights out with Randy and a few of the guys at the station and I intend to keep up with them as they are decent guys and not skirt chasers. We'd usually go to a sports bar, drink a few beers, watch a game or a fight then go home. Occasionally, Randy and I would go to see a shoot-em-up movie the type that Audrey abhors. We usually reserved theatre nights, the ballet, symphony, concerts, gentle movies for couples and I would go even if I didn't have a date. Jill dearest, I just thought of something. How would you like to be ostensibly pregnant at our wedding? Think of it! It's July now and you could be really showing late December. To hell with convention, we're not kids anymore and why wait? When was your last period?

Actually dearest, I hope that you won't be angry with me but I stopped taking the pill after my period two weeks ago.

You sly foxy woman. I love you for being able to read my mind. You must be ovulating——right around——now!!

CHAPTER 4

Hopefully our baby will be born in the spring as in the natural order of life. We will have no mortgage and I have plenty of savings to tide us over for quite some time. Our honeymoon will continue right in our home where you can familiarize me more with the business. We'll chart the projects and I'll be the project manager scheduling in, working with, the suppliers and sub-trades with you inspecting the progress whenever. Do you think that's workable?

Absolutely! It'll enable me to be a stay at home mom. We should discuss how many kids we want, asked Jill.

I feel that if we can manage a boy and a girl in any order, we should stop there. How do you feel about that? My preference would be for a girl first then a boy because she will know her brother better than he knows himself and steer him away from the girls not for him. I'll make certain that he doesn't become sissified not that boys become sissified when they have an older sister. A boy might become over-protective of his younger sister. Those are my initial thoughts.

Fine, said Jill, but what if they are the same sex?

We could discuss it. I'd be open say for one more shot at it if you'd like. Children are our treasures and although two would be more workable at this point in time, we should have as many as we feel that we could nurture lovingly and manage financially.

What will we tell them when they're of the age when they can count months, anniversaries and birth dates?

The truth! That we were in love and didn't want to wait any longer than we had to for their arrival.

Jill giggled coyly. There's no time like the present and don't forget to mark it on our calendar.

CHAPTER 5

Hi Audrey, Randy. Welcome to our home. I trust that you had no trouble getting here. (Randy pretending that he couldn't look Jill in the eyes, held his hand over his eyes).

Randy! joked Jill carrying on with it. It's okay. The coast is clear and the swallows are back at Capistrano.

Jill and Audrey took a quick look at each other sizing each other up then moved quickly to embrace each other firmly. (Tears started).

Jack and Randy hugged firmly— both felt like crying but didn't.

(Elbow to elbow with Audrey, Jill escorted her to the living room. Randy and Jack followed. They each found a comfortable place to sit).

Let me bring in the snacks, said Jill. We can show you around after you've relaxed and eaten.

No honey, interjected Jack quickly. You take it easy, I'll get it.

(This got Audrey's attention. They must have started. Fantastic! They decided not to wait. Why should they? We'll speak in private shortly).

Randy. Want a brew?

Yep!

Let's go into the kitchen.

Jill, what an exquisite home you have. I love what you've done with the decor!

Thank you Audrey. I've studied interior design but it's only a hobby now as I had to concentrate on building my business in order to survive. A farmer friend sold it to me with a minimal down payment and interest only mortgage. Jack will pay off the mortgage when he sells his house or do some fancy financing until it's sold.

What is your business? We know so little about each other and we have so much to learn about each other I'm so excited, said Audrey.

I'm a landscape architect.

Are you pregnant Jill?

I should know shortly. I went off the pill almost one month ago and I should have had my period yesterday. My boobs and nipples just started being tender today like my period. No morning sickness just yet. If I'm pregnant, I'll probably get morning sickness in a few days. Jack didn't want to wait and doesn't care if I'm obviously pregnant when we get married. Why wait? he says, hang convention. I love it! Think about it. I'll be carrying our child! I'll be an expectant bride!

What about you and Randy? What did you work at? You look quite chic.

Randy is an electrical engineer and has his own consulting firm. Has about 10 employees, loves it and is doing okay. I was a fashion designer working for a fashion company in the city until I went on maternity a few months ago. We specialize in plus-size fashions for women and we're quite successful. All our models are plus-sized and they're gorgeous. Major retailers have bought our lines. I almost forgot that we have a line of chic maternity wear as well. Jill dear, when you observe women these days, so many of us are "plus-sized".

Yes! Especially when I examine myself in the mirror.

Enough of that, Jill dear. This is too good to be true. I'm two months pregnant and we're not ready to make any announcements just yet. I started to get morning sickness about one month ago and thankfully, crackers seem to help. But, at times it's not restricted to the morning. Good news though. It's less frequent now even though I read that it could go on for around 14 weeks or so. You might start feeling nauseous as early as the first week or so. My boobs are tender right now and I'll not wear a bra. It's unhealthy. My nipples also feel sore or tingly at times. All this is similar to what happens the night before my period only more dramatic.

It's still a bit early for me to feel any body changes. My next period is due in about one week and hopefully, someone will be talking to me. And when he/she does, I'll use the home test kit followed by a trip to my doctor who delivered me.

Hopefully the two of us will be pregnant and wheeling our babies in prams together when we visit which will be very frequently.

How's Randy reacting to your pregnancy?

He loves it but can't wait to get back in the saddle again—in not on, and you know what I mean. He refuses to while my boobs are tender. He's so concerned and respectful of my condition. I sympathize with him. But I sometimes lend a helpful hand which Randy appreciates.

Jill giggled. It's in their DNA. Amazing these guys and God bless their hormones.

I hear the boys coming back. They must have been yukking it up while in there.

Hey Jill, said Jack, do you know that Audrey and Randy are pregnant.

Isn't that wonderful replied Jill. I told Audrey that we've started.

Boy, you women don't waste time getting to the point. Here are the snacks, said Jack proudly. Just what pregnant ladies need: celery, broccoli florets, carrot sticks, sliced zucchini and a home made dip.

Really! said Audrey. Where's the rum and raisin ice cream?

Oh! Coming up! It's in the freezer. Shall we gild the lily with homemade whipped topping?

Always gild the lily, Jack. Now you're talking, Jack boy. Little one and I will thank you.

(Jack goes and returns with the ice cream, scoop, four bowls, whipped topping and spoons on a serving tray).

Audrey, I can only eat a little as I don't want to put on any additional weight during my pregnancy. I might try to lose about 10 pounds or so through healthy eating but without dieting. Only might, I'll see what my doctor recommends. And I should watch my candida which I have under control. Up to several months ago I had cottage cheese coming out of my vag. Sorry Randy. Women's talk. You just happen to be here.

Love women's talk, Jill.

Randy! said Audrey with a mild joking rebuke.

Anyway, let's enjoy it together. Mmm!. Not quite as good a replacement for sex but still good said Randy with his eyes closed and savouring the ice cream.

Jack, said Audrey, a while ago you started telling Randy how you two met but stopped as you didn't want to take the energy away from when were all to share it. Like tonight?

What were you boys yukking it up about? asked the girls simultaneously.

Randy remembered the time that I peed in my pants.

You what? said Audrey.

I'll explain that one in a bit. Jill hon, would you mind if I start off because my part started before we met.

No, dearest, not at all. Go ahead. I gave up on meeting a man—oh, there was always some hope—long before we met, sighed Jill.

I was dejected, depressed over my social life, lack of a meaningful relationship with a woman with whom to share my life. I wasn't a kid anymore. Then when I heard George Strait sing You're Something Special To Me, the lyrics resonated with me. I stopped writing and took guitar lessons to be able to achieve some competency. Then one starlit Thursday—Thursday, keep that in mind— night a few weeks ago when I was feeling really low and miserable, I sang it out to the universe asking, praying for my soul mate.

Jill, do you want to take it from here?

Sure dearest.

My friend Joan in the city had a fire in her home the next day—Friday— in the morning and Jack, the Assistant Fire Chief, arrived with the engines and the fire was extinguished quickly. He told the men to return the trucks to the station in order to discuss fire safety in the home. Joan found him so nice and without a ring on his finger and asked if he would like go on a blind date with a dear friend—me. Joan is a client and we've been close for years. You'll meet her at our wedding—Jack please mark that on the calendar. I was skeptical of a firefighter because I judged that we would be miles apart culturally, intellectually. Jack may or not know that he taught me, reminded me that one's job doesn't necessarily define that person unless that person wants to be defined by that job. Not at that time but a short while later as I played back the conversation in my mind.

Jack, do you want to continue?

Oh sure, hon. When did that lesson occur?

One of the first things that I said to you was: Oh, you're the firefighter and regretted making that statement immediately.

Jack took over. Yes, I said it purposefully: that's how I earn my living. I made a specific point of saying that and I hadn't realized until now that you picked up my intended meaning. Another reason why I'm nuts about you. Anyway, feeling a little skeptical I decided to get it over with and asked if I could see Jill on Saturday, the first of my five day leave and she accepted. Jill, you take over?

I too felt skeptical as you know the typical guy isn't attracted to fatties and I thought as a macho type of guy you'd be typical although Joan said hat you were well-spoken—I had forgotten that part.

Jack?

On the drive up I kept reminding myself not to get hung up on looks, to determine who the real person was residing inside her skin. When I arrived I was impressed with the landscaping—it was exquisite. I knocked at the door—a wood pecker knocker—and waited. Jill answered. I looked directly at her and was taken by the welcome look in her face, her eyes twinkled and she smiled and sparked. Jill?

Here was this hunk who didn't give me the obvious once, twice over, stopping at my ass. His speech indicated that he was college educated, cultivated, his voice was soft. He had a sensitive, sincere face. He smiled at me, his eyes shone, told me that he was interested in me; told me that the landscaping was exquisite as well as the interior décor when I gave him the tour of the house save for my bedroom. We went for a walk and began to share our lives and discovered that we were both raised by loving single moms. Jack?

We were careful not to walk too close to each other—just a caution. As we were sharing our lives I hadn't noticed that the distance between us was narrowing until we kept bumping into each other and then quickly apologizing for it. You might say that the walk and especially the sharing started to draw us closer to each other.

But the manure fight? And peeing in the pants asked Audrey and Randy together.

Hey Jack, I seem to remember the peeing in the pants now that you mention it. We were double dating and I had my dad's new car.

I'll come to it, guys. Be patient. Let me build it up to a dramatic pitch.

(When Jack told the two stories, purposefully in a droll manner, about the most embarrassing moments in his life, all three were on the floor in hysterics).

As we continued walking I noticed a secluded hut in a clearing.

Jill?

I explained to Jack that it was my private brooding place where I would go when depressed—where I needed to get away from the fast spin of the world, to think things through, to let the mood pass. I was touched when Jack asked for permission to be there with me—he didn't presumptuously barge in. We sat down on my bench, close to each other and didn't say a word. I felt loving energy pouring out of Jack. Then, as though someone choreographed it, we both stood, faced each other and hugged, firmly. Jack?

The energy in there was powerful. I felt its sacredness. At the same time I felt like jumping her but managed, somehow, to control that urge, which believe me was getting very strong. But not in a sacred place.

Jill?

I felt that way too and I took him by the hand to the drive shed where—yes—the manure was delivered that morning. Wanted to see whether he was a prissy city boy, you know the type. Oooh! Horse manure!

Oh, said Jack. You were testing me? Sly cagey one!

Well, I purposefully walked into it across the shed to the other side pretending to look out the window but really, to get his reaction. And boy did I get it. He shocked me when he heaved a horse ball at my waist. When I quickly recovered from the shock and knew the game, I flung some at him. Then we kept at it for a short while—we were in hysterics— then stopped in the middle of the pile to hug and kiss each other.

Jack?

That was the defining moment in our budding relationship. There are times when if there is a more profound meaning to an activity it dawns on me later.

Jack dearest. What profundity did you derive from it?

There are times that we create our own metaphors and don't realize it at that time. It dawned on me last week. If we can endure a horse manure fight, we should be able to endure most of what life can toss at us.

Wow! said Randy. Deep shit thinking, Jack.

Jill?

Oh yes! Although I was sure by this time that Jack wasn't in for a one night stand I felt that I should give him the sincerity challenge, the testosterone challenge…(Jack jumps in)

The what challenge?

Dear, the testosterone challenge. By asking him, in the manure pile, if he would like to spend the night. I usually put it to guys who if accepted, I'd use my back out plan. But never in my life did I ever imagine asking someone to spend the night with me standing in a manure pile.

A green manure pile, interjected Jack.

When I tried it with Jack I suddenly felt ambivalent: I was so attracted to him that I wanted and hoped that he'd say yes. But if I did would I be rushing things prematurely? if he said no, I'd be very hurt. Well Jack refused in a manner that made me want him even more. Jack?

Were the tests over, hon? Anyway. I remember it perfectly to the word. When you asked me, I slowly and gently released myself from the hug, held you at arms length, looked into your eyes, let he blood return to my head, gathered my thoughts and said—I was really serious: yes and no. Yes! I'm quite attracted to you and you know it. Under other circumstances I would have gladly said yes and as I've been there before. No because I need and want to know you better, that what we feel for each other is genuine and not as a result of a turn on. You're a gem and I don't want to mess things up. I know that you're not a loose woman and you're just as much turned on to me as I to you. Intimacy will draw me closer to you and want to know and feel that it would be reciprocated. I don't want to suppress my emotions during intimacy. If I love you I will tell you that not only during periods of intimacy but at other times as well. Also, not while were both smelling and covered with manure and we don't know each other well enough to shower together. But if it's not too late, how about a cup of tea. Or if it's too late how about a juicy passionate kiss to remember you by until we next get together.

Well, Jill herded me to the wall, planted one kiss on me, ran her knee up to my crotch that buckled my knees and gave me something that lasted until I got home... and beyond.

Randy nodded knowingly.

How touching and strong of you Jack, to control your hormones until you got home, said Audrey with a sympathetic smile.

Oh what a waste, said Jill. with her eyes closed imagining what could have been during that session.

Randy, said Jill, what was Jack like as a teenager?

He was fun to be with—spontaneous, witty, original. Didn't date much as he had to work after school to help out financially but he did participate in extra-curricular school sports especially football, gymnastics, some boxing and hockey. He was a brilliant scholar and had to concentrate on his studies in order to obtain scholarships otherwise he would have to alternate work and college which would have taken him years to obtain his degrees. I remember that essay you wrote wherein you took a whack at the fashion industry when we were teens. Audrey, you'll love this. Our English teacher, Miss Garbeau, asked us to write a poem or essay and were given several subjects and we were to chose the one about which we were passionate. One of the subjects was the fashion industry which she assumed that the girls would use, one of several others could have been motorcycle and or vehicle maintenance and the like for the guys plus one topic of your own choosing. Do you remember your essay, Jack?

Jack began to laugh, composed himself and said let me give you the background to this. Mom loved fashion catalogues especially vintage ones. As a teenage boy, I'd sneak into the toilet —Jill and Audrey started to giggle— and, you know—study them.

Creep!, said the girls in unison.

I knew that if I bought a Playboy or Hustler, mom surely would have discovered it under my mattress. Then one rainy day I discovered garter belts in one of those old catalogues which for some reason really turned me on and on and on. Wow!

Creep! joked Jill.

Then when the class was given the option of an essay or poem and the fashion industry the idea came to me in a flash and I decided on a poem. It just flowed and in about 30 minutes had finished it and titled it initially Obsession but decided to title it Ode to Garter Belts. I was very close with Miss Garbeau—I would call her my mentor— and although I was pushing her boundaries with this, I was passionate about it and hoped that she would feel my passion and that it wouldn't go any further than her. That she'd mark it and return it to me.

Do you remember the poem? asked Randy.

Do I? Sure, but not to recite from memory. I have it backed up in the office. But I certainly remember the "fallout".

Fallout? asked the girls.

Yah, fallout. I'll explain shortly.

Please retrieve it asked Audrey. Garter belts? They made a short-lived comeback a few decades ago, I believe.

Let me check. I transferred everything to CD's. Back in a Jiff.

Jill, said Randy, wait until you hear this poem. I won't tell you the reaction, the fallout Jack got from various sectors in the school but you'll gain a new respect for his erudition, wit, sincerity, passion and courage.

Here it is, said Jack carrying in his laptop.

Well, Miss Garbeau praised the class for the quality of their efforts. "As you all know, pupils, Jack is one of the school's top scholars and will pursue Honour English at college and I will give him the best reference that I can falling short of hyperbole. His graduation picture will hang in Rogue's Gallery along with our top scholars of past years. Jack, please come up here and read your poem to the class. Your passion for the subject was so palpable that even I felt it. Jack, come up here to the front of the class". "Come".

Do I really have to? It's really very personal.

"That's why you should be proud to share it with your classmates whom you will in all probability never see again after graduation—save for Commencement—something for them to remember you by".

My knees felt weak and I felt like throwing up as I walked to the front of the class and to the side of her desk.

"Class. I gave Jack 100% for this poem. Here's it is Jack. Take your time then start anytime" then leaned back in her chair.

I was crimson with mortification, had I been standing on kindling I felt that I would have surely ignited it. Then with a dry mouth I began:

Ode To Garter Belts
Garter belt garter belt
Circling o'er the Promised Land
Invited to enter, too shy to take a stand
Entered via my trusty right hand.
Garter belt garter belt

Suspended o'er feminine thighs
Of gorgeous models emphasizing their Y's
Short ones, zuftig ones—unimportant their size.
Garter belt garter belt
Why, did you go out of fashion?
You certainly aroused my teenage passion.
Crusted underpants and bed sheets
for my dear mother's wash session.
Garter belt garter belt
Naughty girls at parties would adjust them
Pretending us guys wouldn't notice them.
Had to wear two jock straps
to safely dance close to them
Garter belt garter belt
Sensuous garment atavistic
Arousing prurience, concupiscence and of course
feelings mystique.
Undoing those clasps made my testes go ballistic.
So fashion gurus wherever you are
Aren't garter belts sexier than panty hose by far?
I realize that panty hose are practical and of this era.
But wow! Undoing those clasps and etc. etc.
So I challenge you all to bring back them back into
fashion
To remind us all of our grandparent's passion.

The girls were struck dumb as Jack waited for their reaction. Then simultaneously they burst out in hysterics as did Randy.

What happened? said the girls after they composed themselves.

First the girls started giggling, then laughing hysterically. The guys were yelling: "hey stud, never knew that you were a wanker".

The bell rang and as the class was leaving Miss Garbeau asked me to remain—it was the final class of the day.

Jack. You're the boldest, most imaginative creative writer that I've ever had in my classes and you know it because I've told you this over the years. If I had a son, I would want him to be like you. You also knew that you were pushing my boundaries. I too have a warped sense of humour and you'll look back at this fondly. I sent your poem plus your other writings, to the Dean of Arts at the college who is a long-time personal friend and I'm certain that you will be on full-scholarship when you go. Never stop writing. You're bold, creative, literate and passionate.

The poem got out all over the school. Since I was a good athlete and one of the guys it blew over pretty fast. As it did with the girls. Anyway, said Jack, changing the subject, if we're finished with the snacks shall we tour the property? We'll use the golf cart, Audrey.

Have to take a loo break first, said Audrey. Me next said Jill.

Jill showed them a Japanese garden and a permaculture project that she was working on. They drove along the path in the wooded area where their hut was.

Jill, Isn't that hut out of character with your other projects, your business?, said Audrey.

It was on the farm when I bought it and thought of razing it. But when I went inside I immediately felt an energy a vibration different from other parts of the farm and other parts of the area. As well, the structure was strong, sound, solidly constructed. There was a wood bench someone had left in there. I sat down. I was depressed at the time—not the usual phenomenon. I felt lonely, wanted a decent man in my life. I remained there for several hours and something made me feel much better. No, I didn't receive a message of self-assurance. Just felt better being there, helped that feeling pass. It became my sacred sanctum.

(They toured the farm and returned to the house. They all had dinner which Jack prepared: roast beef, scalloped potatoes, steamed baby carrots and a fresh garden salad with an oil and vinegar dressing. Then tea and instead of pastry, Jack served anise).

When I was invited to dinner by one of the men at the station who had Italian ancestry, they served anise instead of pastry. They were both lean and healthy. I never forgot that. Just a basic meal that mom, by necessity, taught me.

Jack, said Randy. It's getting late and it's a long drive back to the city. We're having fun especially with you filling Jill in on your past notoriety.

Please stay over tonight, said Jill, and have breakfast with us and then enjoy the scenic trip back home.

We'd love to, said Audrey.

Here's the guest room. We share the loo. When it's closed, we assume that it's in use as there's no lock on the door. A night-light will be on. Here are some tooth brushes. We don't use commercial toothpaste, instead we make a paste from non-aluminized baking soda and hydrogen peroxide. They're on this shelf with a mixing bowl and spoon.

In bed: Randy, Jill is a sweet heart and I'm so very happy for them. When was the last time that you saw him beaming, genuinely happy? And Jill! She so alive! And we're open with each other. I'm so excited having met her! We enjoyed each others company and will be close. As you are with Jack.

For life, said Randy.

In bed: They are a terrific couple and looking forward to spending more time with Audrey. I'm so excited having met her! She's a gem and I enjoyed talking to her as I feel that she does with me and we'll be close. And you and Randy are so close. Jack dear, I never knew that you were such a creative writer.

Jill, hon. You'll learn a lot more pretty soon. I'm sure

that Randy will mention the safe sex manual that I was asked to write for the school year book.

You're joking?

I won't tell you about it now as I want to keep it fresh if Randy wants me to talk about it tomorrow. Otherwise, some other time.

I'm curious, dear.

Anyway, said Jack, embracing Jill and kissing her. Hon, the thought occurred to me. We haven't discussed an engagement ring?

I never thought about it, dear. Let me think.

(Jill takes a few seconds). No! I don't want an engagement ring but when we're in the city, let's buy two gold wedding bands. I don't have the need of flashing a diamond—perhaps if I were younger and the wedding was a long way off. Jack dear, the wedding is five months away, I expect to be five months pregnant and showing. As you said: hang convention. I'm not one for jewelry, Jack. But perhaps one day in our travels if I see one that resonates with me, you'll surprise me with it after I drop a few hints.

Yes, drop hints as I detest jewelry, never ever think about it and please, drop hints.

Dearest, what you're telling me is that you don't consider the gold wedding band as jewelry but as a symbol of our commitment to each other?

I love you Jill, for your insights and understanding. I'm rolling over to sleep but I won't fart this time.

I'm grateful. But the window remains open and the fan is on the sill just the same.

Jill puts her arm over Jack to sleep spoon and Jack takes her hand.

(Next morning and Jack and Jill are in the kitchen).

I'll start the coffee, said Jack, I hear them moving around.

Jack dear, please get the turkey bacon and eggs from the fridge in the pantry.

Jill prepares the table. Jack returns and hugs Jill. We've started entertaining as a couple. I'm happy doing this together.

You're happy? I'm absolutely in heaven and kisses him with her leg moving slowly up his crotch. (Jack's knees were about to buckle as Audrey and Randy emerge from their room).

Oh! Didn't mean to interrupt.

Just a moment's interlude, said Jill.

Audrey, what would you like to drink? Randy you're black, first thing.

Jack, if you have some hot green tea, I'd love some, asked Audrey.

Coming up guys and goes into the kitchen leaving Jill with them.

Audrey, what do you eat for breakfast?

If you have Melba Toast, Rye crackers, soda crackers and the like? I'll try one piece of crisp bacon.

It's turkey bacon without nitrates. Is that okay Audrey?

Yes it is said Audrey appreciatively.

You Randy?

Audrey sweetheart, if it doesn't nauseate you: crisp turkey bacon, eggs sunny side up, rye toast and butter.

No dear, it won't.

Jack returns with the tea and coffee. Jill brings the food in on a tray and the conversation begins.

Audrey. If it's okay with you, are the two of us allowed to visit your office? If I'm pregnant and I think that I am, I'd like to buy a few outfits and it will be our first shopping spree together.

I'd love that. Just let me know when.

Jack, remember the safe sex guide that you wrote for the

year book that caused lots of flack for the principal when some parents objected to it? But he rode through it okay.

Jack looks at Jill. Randy, I knew that you were going to bring that up. Okay, let me bring in my laptop.

My, I'm certainly learning a lot about my Jack. Still waters sure run deep. There's a crazy side to him that I adore. Did he ever tell you about the strip dance that he did at the Redneck Review a few weeks ago.

Jack did what? said Audrey and Randy laughing but in disbelief.

(Redneck Review, said Randy to himself and made a mental note of it).

Okay, says Jack bringing in his laptop. Are you ready?

Miss Garbeau asked me to write a manual on safe sex near the end of my final year because there were a few early-teen pregnancies in our school. She confided in me that Mr. Graham (the principal) was just as warped and wacky and she and had managed to convince him that I should write a manual on safe sex for the pupils. A manual like no other manual that the pupils would relate to knowing that it came from me: "especially with your reputation as sexual sophisticate".

That hurts Miss Garbeau, I remember saying to her.

"Jack, don't feel pressured. Give it some thought". She gave about three months or so. Well, here it is, what you've been all waiting for, said Jack proudly.

I titled it: safe sox. A manual of practice for novices and others

By request from official sources, I have written a guide intended primarily for a female who has started Matriculating, a young male capable of achieving a Vector and for the Old & Listless (O&L) achieving a Vector Newman. A Vector Newman also applies to both young and elderly males at the moment of Ejacupation.

Although there are a plethora of guides on this subject, this guide uses simple familiar terminology.

The act of Safe Sox is referred to as Coagulation and occurs in a device called a Co-agulator (Co-ag).

PREVENTION—LOSS OF SOX

Prior to Coagulation, the participating couple must consider prevention, loss of sox and additional, unexpected Sox emanating from unknown sources.

One method would be, prior to placing Sox in the Co-ag, for the male to use a Condomnation, the female, a Contradeceptive agent—contravallation in the UK—all available in your local pharmacy. One potential "side-effect" for the female could be a skipped cycle of the Co-ag causing temporary upset to her parents who entrusted her with Safe Sox. Prolonged use of a Contradeceptive agent—contravallation in the UK—could make the Co-ag lazy. Discuss this with a counselor specializing in lazy Co-ags. Males generally consider don't like Condomnations.

An inexpensive method is to place the Sox in a protective sheath bag—such as a cozy capote— before placing in the Co-ag. A zippered mesh bag only serves to keep Sox together and little else.

Whatever the method, it must be implicitly and explicitly agreed upon beforehand.

Forshpice—Pre and Post-Treatment of Safe Sox

Once prevention is decided upon there is the need of Forshpice.

There are several approaches to Forshpice— the Classic and the Romantic.

In the Classic mode where structure, form and

exactitude are required, it could be as simple, immediate and understood as an unmistakable elbow in your partner's rib: "are you ready for Safe Sox"? The Romantic approach, where structure, form and exactitude are subordinated to intent, there is to be a demonstrated gentleness—a respect for Safe Sox. This can be a caressing, smoothing prior to placement into the Co-ag. Background music would enhance the environment. Regardless of which method is selected, a mutual pre-wash of Sox is recommended especially at the end of a difficult day, after a strenuous hi-impact aerobic class or coming off a 12 hour shift in a coal mine in mid-July. To add life and colour to the load, consider adding a sprig of kale. Don't forget to add some fodder as a stabilizer.

After Safe Sox and removal from the Co-ag, it is recommended to continue with Forshpice— remove the Sox from the Co-ag, and again, smoothing them before returning them back to their places.

TROUBLE SHOOTING GUIDE-NOVICES

(1) (a) The participating male loses his Vector.

DO NOT PANIC!!
or blame yourself. Stop the Co-ag. Relax, review and consider. Consider hand washing the Sox thereby eliminating the pressure, tension and salvaging the procedure. Consider continuing with Forshpice. Or try again soon, perhaps this wasn't your day.

(b) Try pleasant visualizations.

(2) The protective sheath—the cozy capote—breaks in the Co-ag.

STOP COAGULATION IMMEDIATELY

and withdraw from Safe Sox by a method known as Soxus Interruptus. Devout Roman Catholics are enjoined to use this method occasionally.

Females should go to their didets immediately in order to woosh.

Care must be taken to ensure that strands from each Sox not become intermingled. If the intermingling is allowed to continue, the agitation of the Co-ag could cause the strands to multiply and twist in processes called Mysoxis and Mytsoxis resulting in either a desirable or undesirable by-product. It just might mess things up.

Trouble Shooting—Experienced Sox Washers

Males. Loss of desire for Safe Sox, unable to achieve a Vector or Vector Newman. Also known as the Dead Bic Syndrome (DBS) named after Bic lighters which fail to function both as advertised and expected. Extremely frustrating to both parties and embarrassing especially to a male in his attempt to locate and gain entry to the fuse box in the dark. An embarrassment to the Bic Corporation as well.

(1) Short-term: Pleasant visualization is highly recommended. As well, consider the use of Argaiv, a substance commonly found your local pharmacy or in an advanced chemset; which will provide a catalytic reaction to the process in the Co- ag. Although outside the terms of reference for this manual, Argaiv can be administered to men in nursing homes in order to prevent them from falling out of their beds at night.

(2) Long-term: Seek the advice and counselling of a female Safe Sox facilitator.

Loss of desire—female.

(1) Short-term: Review Safe Sox procedure especially Forshpice. If the   Classic was used without success, the Romantic should be considered.

(2) Long-term: Check the oil in the bearings and the inner linings of the hoses—it could be that an oil and lube is required, or that different brands should be experimented with. If that fails, call your handyman. This could be the reason for your feelings of Grigidity

TROUBLESHOOTING—ALL USERS

Fallout. The door to the Co-ag permitted the sox to Fallout—very upsetting. This requires a rapid "all hands on deck" approach immediately to resume the process, perhaps "taking it from the top".

NEVER

(1) NEVER, especially males, ask whether the experience was enjoyable immediately at the conclusion as it implies that "you were not there"—where were you!? Spiritual teaching requires that you be " in the moment". Forget about your hairdressing appointment, your pajama party with the girls Friday night, the need to polish the chrome on your car, that Identity problem in Trig —admittedly and with humility, I admonish myself for forgetting this latter Never. Always be there!

However, a post-mortem is welcome when a state of objectivity returns, the Sox have been returned and the good, the bad the ugly evaluated.

(2) NEVER use Saran Wrap with a twist-tie, a Zip or Slide Lock bag in the Co-ag. due to the intense temperature and agitation in the Co-ag.

Remember to drink fluids and to eat a healthy meal following especially a salad. For practicing Roman Catholics, you can revive the sprig of kale and fodder for your salad by saying three kale Marys and two our fodders.

Respectfully,

Jack. Graduating Class of 1998

Jill Audrey and Randy were speechless.

Continuing quickly: I told Miss Garbeau that after I had researched several self-help type manuals and articles on prevention of unwanted pregnancies, I decided to address it to adults as well. Why? you or Mr. Graham might ask Because adults should consider these issues as well. When I began reading it I saw I slight smile at the corner of Miss Garbeau's mouth which she suppressed. The smile and suppression continued. Then I saw slight heaving of her slim belly throughout—a chuckle—I believe.

"Jack! Original, bold, in-your-face, funny, creative, irreverent. I'll discuss this with Mr. Graham. Oh, by the way! A friend tells me that on occasion her special friend suffers from what did you call it: Dead Bic Syndrome? That when it doesn't function in the dark as advertised and expected they are very upset, frustrated, embarrassed, especially when the male tries to locate and enter the fuse box in the dark"?

"Why thank you Miss Garbeau, I said with pride, for the encouragement and critique. I hope that, if published, that it would have an impact on the reader".

"I'm certain that it will, she said. And on certain others as well".

Jack, that manual was hilarious, said Jill. You've got to continue writing.

Audrey and Randy were still laughing—Randy gently nudging Audrey with an "I told you so".

I certainly will, hon, after we organize ourselves. Perhaps I might write about us: how we met, shared a lot about our lives, fell in love, had a manure fight. Hon, everybody has a story and ours is unique. In fact, not just me, we'll write it together for the benefit of our children.

This has been a fantastic visit, said Audrey. Jill dear, please let us know the results as soon as you can and I'm looking forward to our first shopping spree.

Jack and Randy hugged each other, Randy giving Jack a gentle jab in the gut.

Jill had tears as they drove off and Jack had his arm around her waist as they both waved goodbye.

Jack dearest, I may be pregnant as I should have had my period today. I'm going to buy a home testing kit tomorrow and if I'm pregnant, make an appointment with Dr. Brown who delivered me.

How wonderful. We'll go to town together say after we visit the mall project?

Perfect!

CHAPTER 6

(Sunday about one hour after Audrey and Randy drove home. The knocker almost bore a hole in the door. The girls barged in).

Where are you two love birds? they all said in unison.

Jill, called Jack from the commode. See who's there. I'm constipated. Not enough fibre and drinking water especially when doing the outdoor physical work. Oh well, my body' is speaking to me. Please tell them I'll be there anon. We weren't expecting them. What's up?

I don't know dear.

Jack will join us shortly. Come in the kitchen while I prepare some coffee, tea.

We haven't spoken to each other in a few days, said Carol, and were concerned.

Let's get comfortable and I'll fill you all in, said Jill as she poured tea while all were seated.

We're all ears said Kate.

Now, where shall I begin, said Jill pretending to give thought to the matter. (Said quickly and excitedly) We're getting married December 15th and you're all my bridesmaids.

Oh Jill, we're all so happy for you and excited. Jack is a gem.

And quite a stripper too, said Kate with a feigned lusty look.

Another thing, said Jill, as she looked around the room pretending that there were outside listeners: (said quickly) I think that I'm pregnant and if I am will buy a home test kit tomorrow and then visit Dr. Brown.

Oh, is that why you're getting married?

No! Not at all. Jack—he really has an unconventional off-the-wall sense of humour as you all should know by now said to me: Jill, let's hang convention. We're not kids and why should we wait? It would be a hoot if you're an obviously five months pregnant bride when we get married. Can you just hear the pastor asking: Jack, do you take Jill, your five month gone expectant bride as your wife?

They all giggled and hugged Jill.

We're so happy for you and Jack, said Kate.

As a theme, you should have posters of shotguns all over, said Sally.

(More giggles).

No bridesmaid dresses, no matching and colour co-ordinated outfits. Just wear something that you'd like to wear. We want it simple and unpretentious. Would any of you feel insulted if I asked Beatrice to be my Maid of Honour?

They looked at each other then said no of course not!

Actually it makes sense because if you chose one of us, then some of us, maybe, would have our noses out of joint.

Beatrice is like a younger sister and Jack and I are trying to fix her up with a young man similarly handicapped. We haven't had the time to check out a few details. But we will.

Hi girls, said Jack as he came in and kissed Jill.

Get a load off your mind, Jack? they asked in unison.

Yes! Thank you for asking, girls. I'm glad that you're all interested in colon motility.

We heard the wonderful news about your wedding and Jill's possible pregnancy and we're so excited and happy for the both of you, said Carol.

Jill, we're thinking of hosting a bridal shower for you. How do you feel about that?

Girls, we've known each other since kindergarten, shared lots of joys and heartaches over the years what with the breakups, make-ups, kids, hirings, firings, divorces and I really appreciate your offer. But no! Jack and I have all that we need. What I really would like is to be able to spend quality time with each other—just us. Let's have a night out just before the wedding. Say! Why not the Redneck Review? Those gorgeous male strippers are still there.

Hey girls, Jack interjected, great idea. Meet here. I can rent a limo to drive you there and back so that you can get pissed without worrying how to get home. Then sleep it off here.

We'll consider it, Jack, said Sally.

Anyway, we've got to go, tomorrow is a work day. Keep us informed. We love you both.

(In bed: Jack gets emotional, sitting up). My father left many years ago and I hardly remember him. I never knew what it's like to have a father to relate to… to discuss common interests, give boundaries, discipline me, hug me, go to sporting events together and cheer for our team… camp out, fish, show him my school marks and simply have a father and son relationship. To introduce him to my friends (tears start)—hey guys, here's my dad. Over the years, I've wanted a family… to be a good husband and father to my children…to give them what I missed plus some. To be active in the raising of my children. To bond with them, give them love, spiritual values, respect for life, a work ethic and more. I want that for us, Jill dearest. To work together in the business, to raise a family and to make a good life for us.

Jill with tears. Hug me hard, dearest. Hug me.

CHAPTER 7

Hi Honey, don't get up. Here are some crackers. The home test kit and morning sickness are proof positive.

That was thoughtful of you sweetheart. Come, sit here beside me. Yes! I've just started with my morning sickness and thankfully, crackers work for me.

Remember hon, when we first made breakfast together I asked you how you liked your eggs? Remember what you told me?

Jiggle giggled: Unfertilized! (said together).

We should start getting dressed as we have a 9:00AM appointment with Dr. Brown, said Jack. I'm so excited!

So am I dearest. I never imagined that I'd ever be pregnant let alone being married. Or being five months pregnant at my wedding. A girl never dreams of that situation. Of that I'm fairly certain.

Well hon, we're living that dream. We'll visit the mall project after Dr. Brown.

Imagine all that happened in 10 days. We really lived your essay said Jill.

Not purposefully, said Jack. My essay was simply a general guide—Part 1 came to me in a dream that I quickly wrote down then expanded it while lying in bed. It's how I imagined life would be living with a woman and not be influenced by male immaturity that the media tries to foist off as being typically male.

Here hon, give me your hand and I'll help you up.

Jack dear. If I'm pregnant, it's only been about 7-10 days. I love that you're so concerned, so doting.

CHAPTER 8

Jill, it's so good to see you said Nancy, Dr Brown's long-time nurse and receptionist leaving her desk and hugging Jill. And you must be Jack giving him the once over.

You got it!

Go right into the Doctor's office as he's expecting you and excited.

Jill dear, I'm absolutely thrilled and happy for you and Jack. Jack, are you okay being here while I give Jill a pelvic exam?

Thanks for asking Dr. Brown. I'm okay with it and intend to be with Jill when she delivers.

Good stuff, Jack.

(Finishes his exam and blood draw).

The results will be back in a few days and Nancy will call you with the results and to schedule appointments.

CHAPTER 9

Sophie, Amos. Welcome to our home.

(Jack and Amos embrace as do Sophie and Jill).

Are you up to be given the grand tour or would you prefer to rest before? asked Jack.

Jack dear, if you don't mind, I'd rather rest first—I'm not the spry gal that I was few years ago. Arthritis has been bothering me lately.

Please have a seat in the living room. (Jack escorts Sophie to a comfortable upholstered chair. Jill escorts Amos, elbow to elbow as well).

Let me bring out some refreshments said Jack. Let's see. Sophie—no wheat, dairy or sugar. Correct?

Yes dear, said Sophie. Thank you for remembering.

I'd never forget that. I've prepared something special. Be back in a jiff.

Jill, we're so happy for you and Jack who's been like a son that we've never had, said Sophie with a few tears. We have three daughters that Jack dated occasionally but only as friends. Platonic is the word they used. If they didn't have a date, Jack would arrange to go. They're all great friends and expect a personal invitation from Jack or else all three will stick a pin, you know where they all said, into his effigy.

Sophie, Amos, I'll personally make certain that Jack delivers the invites, said Jill with a feigned wince. Jack has a great memory and doesn't forget friends. We haven't started compiling our invitation list. We plan on having our wedding here on Sunday December 15th come rain, snow or sun, in an enormous tent that we will rent. It'll be potluck.

Yes, said Amos. We knew that Jack wanted to get married but it never worked out. And we're absolutely thrilled that you found each other.

Tell me quickly before Jack comes back: what were they like.

Sophie jumps in: like Barbie dolls. Some had brains to match, others didn't. I think that he brought them to our affairs as arm pieces so that the married men's eyes would pop and they would pester him for the details back at the station.

Yep, said Amos, stretching his legs on the recliner with hands behind his head, smiling: yes! Jack had all our attention back at the station.

Amos, yours too? asked Sophie surprised.

(Amos, caught off guard). Ahem, well when I had to be there as Chief to discuss station matters. I couldn't barge in and ask them to stand at attention. Of course, I listened politely until Jack finished, then started the meeting.

Well done, applauded Sophie. Dear, you're still fast on your feet and I love you for it.

Jill clapped her hands and laughed with them.

(Jack comes in). I've made a non-dairy chocolate and strawberry ice cream snack sweetened with stevia. The ingredients are unsalted roasted cashews, unsweetened coca powder for the chocolate, almond oil, vanilla extract and the stevia. The strawberries are organic and the recipe is the same as the chocolate save for the cocoa. As well, we have a selection of organic coffees-caf and decaf—herbal teas as well as organic green tea. I can ice the tea and coffee. We also have a choice of wheat and gluten free muffins—blueberry or cranberry.

How thoughtful of you Jack, said Sophie and Amos together.

Iced green tea for both of us would be fine, said Sophie.

Same for us? said Jack, looking at Jill, who smiled and nodded.

(After the snacks, they all had seconds, Jack spoke). Sophie, Amos, you've been like parents to me who welcomed me into your family along with three gorgeous daughters who educated me like big sisters as to the —"ways of women"?—so to speak.

(Sophie nodded as she and the girls would talk).

And I'm especially grateful that you'll marry us as there is no one else on this planet that I would want. Jill and I are very much in love, we're not kids anymore and want to start a family ASAP and we've been trying. Would you feel awkward, have second thoughts, about marrying us if Jill were ostensibly pregnant? We're not getting married because Jill is pregnant.

Jack dear, you of course wouldn't have known this but Amos and I were also very much in love and I was three months pregnant when we decided to elope. Amos?

Jack, son. It would be my pleasure.

Thank you said Jack and Jill together, relieved.

And I'll deal with your daughters at the wedding especially when Jill is blooming, added Jack.

They'll love it said Sophie.

(After the tour they all hugged and Sophie and Amos drove off.

They're such dear couple said Jill).

Come on. Let's go to bed.

Gee honey now that you're pregnant I won't be able to experience any of your period moods. Boy did I ever with Sophie's and Amos' daughters.

I'm not too bad, dear.

Hon, if no one is around it's a non event. Women simply get on with their day despite the discomfort. When a man is around, he gets the full impact so that he feels it—or something close; doesn't get off Scot free. That's what men are for. Mom used to howl at a comic strip called Hi and Lois, I believe. Lois would break a plate over Hi's head—you'd see the shards flying all over the kitchen—when life was closing in on her. After she smashed the plate, Hi would say something like: "there there dear. Do you feel better now?

Honey, when you get your period, you have my permission to break a plate over my head. To change the subject: do you remember that presentable young man that we saw at the jamboree that Beatrice likes? She blushed when they spoke.

Yes, dear. His name is Allan. Why?

Evidently he works at Mack's Garden Centre. He's the one that I worked with a few days ago. He's bright and capable, accompanies the men on the truck and helps them plant flowers especially for senior citizens who are unable to do so. Let's play cupid. We'll buy flowers to plant around the side of the house—you chose them as I'm not knowledgeable with flowers but will be—give me time. Invite Beatrice over to help with dinner and when Allan and I finish planting, I'll invite him in for dinner then drive him home. I'll explain our little plan to Mack. How does this sit with you?

Let's go for it, dear!

He also likes music, to sing and poetry.

Aha! said Jill. Do I smell a performance for Beatrice?

Perhaps! Oh, I forgot. Did you find out whether she's on birth control pills or had a tubal ligation?

She had a tubal years before we became friends. I'll check with her and ask how she'll feel being my Maid of honour.

Jack dear, why the urgency about Beatrice's birth control?

Well hon, from my experience with high functioning handicapped they're really into sex—hot stuff when they're turned on. They suppress nothing. They could easily go at it the first moment they have of privacy.

Sounds pretty normal to me dearest. Have you coached them? joked Jill.

Hon, I would be concerned about a pregnancy. All kidding aside, they're not going to stop and ask what birth control measures each have taken. Can you just picture Beatrice holding a naked Allan apart and asking: by the way do you have a condom or had a vasectomy? I want them to develop a loving relationship without Beatrice being pressured by others into having a therapeutic abortion.

I should have known that, dearest. That's the only reason that I love you. No other.

Come here you sexy and pregnant woman. Now that you're pregnant, I need to be told more than ever that you love me. A guy needs to be held and given that assurance.

Jill giggled and gave Jack that deep sensuous gaze.

Hey, why are you removing my jockey shorts? Help. Mommy.

CHAPTER 10

Hi Jill, said a happy Nancy, you're pregnant all right. Remind Jack to buy a carload of crackers for you.

(Jill in tears). Thank you Nancy, I'll tell Jack when he returns from the mall. He's taken over the management of the project as though he were in the business for years.

Jill dear, where in the world did you find him? My daughter—you know Gillian—is intelligent, attractive, accomplished but can't seem to find a worthwhile beau so she's having an affair with a married man in the city. It pains me but, I guess, it keeps her satisfied at one level knowing that she's accepting second best. A human needs the touch, the affection of another human and this is her way of satisfying that need. My concern is not one of judgment but how will she be able to meet a decent single man. Waiting for her cell phone to ring for the time when he's available.

Nancy, I just thought of something. Why don't you and Gillian come to our wedding December 15th. Jack is inviting his former fireman friends and some are single and decent guys as Jack describes them.

I'll ask Gillian but I don't think that she'll want to date a fireman as she has dated professionals, business men and the like.

Nancy, I had the same notions, reservations before I met Jack. I initially said, when he called: oh! You're the fireman and you know how Jack responded?

No! How?

That's how I earn my living. He explained why he said that later on when we were committed: that one's job doesn't necessarily define them unless of course they want their job to define them or someone else wants to label them. From my experience, someone with limited vision needs to put a label on a person in order to "understand" them according to their mental check list or agenda. I used to read it on men's faces as we would talk—how can I label her? Jack was a brilliant student and had to get employment to help his mom who was diagnosed with cancer. Being a fireman provided him with a medical plan, a good income, pension, with plenty of time to write. I'm not saying that Gillian will find a fireman to her liking. I'm simply saying that she should keep her options open and investigate other avenues of meeting men. Please tell her this and I expect her to RSVP me or I'll plant poison ivy in her garden.

They both laughed. I'll see her there even if I have to drag her there.

Oh, Jack has just driven in. Got to go and give him a special welcome home with the news. Thanks again, Nancy, I'll book in with Dr. Brown shortly.

Hi dearest! Jill pushes Jack against the wall, runs her knee up Jack's crotch and plants a kiss on him. Jack's knees buckle.

Jack composing himself. Jill honey, I used to spar a bit in college with some hard hitters, caught a few good ones in my time, but no one ever buckles my knees the way you hit me. I love it!

Dearest, we're pregnant!

Jack tosses his peak cap away and swings Jill around then stops because he feels that Jill could be delicate. How wonderful honey. (Tears start, then composes himself). I gave up hope of ever becoming a father, having a home with a loving wife and kids. Not only do we have a home, we'll also have kids and work together in the same business and I'm loving it working my butt off with you. We'll continue to develop a local business with a reputation for creativity and ethics.

How did it go today? You look a bit weary.

When Mack's truck didn't show up on time, I called and found out that their driver was sick so I drove over, picked up Allan—I'll come to him shortly—and drove to the mall to help him plant the bushes and trees and they look great. I also had a good discussion with Allan, not the first one either. He likes Beatrice but is too shy to ask her out. I'm not pushing, hon, but were you able to find out about Beatrice?

Yes dear, thanks for reminding me. A tubal about five years ago.

Wonderful! Now we can play cupid. We have a few more bushes and trees to lay out. If you invite Beatrice for dinner, then instead of driving Allan directly home I'll invite him for dinner.

Sounds good, Eros. I'll call her now. Why not take your shower and when you come out, I'll know whether she'll be available.

(Jack embracing Jill with his hands on her butt). Come in with me gorgeous. I need my—back and a few other parts—scrubbed. I'm certain that you need a few—parts—scrubbed as well. Then call.

Beast!

CHAPTER 11

Say Allan, how about dinner at our place. I'm hungry and it's a long drive to your place.

Thank you, Jack. What's cooking?

Don't know. Jill and Beatrice are preparing a dinner for us two hard working guys. Come in and take a shower—there's one in the basement with lots of towels. We must be clean and handsome for the girls.

Did you say Beatrice is there?, whispered Allan slightly flushed.

Yes. She and Jill are good friends and they always cook dinner together on this day. There's always plenty of food.

I like Beatrice.

(Arriving home) Hey dearest. Jack kisses Jill and whispers, watch the knee honey, Allan is observing.

Jill giggles. Why not let him learn something?

Teach Beatrice.

Allan, that good-looking woman in the red apron is Beatrice. Beatrice, do you know this handsome young man? His name is Allan Do you know each other?

(Both nod with a blush and glance at the floor).

Men! Hard working men of the field. Sit down anywhere, announced Jill.

We sure put in a long hard day planting the last of the bushes and trees in the Eastern sector. Right on schedule which pleased the Project Manager. Allan, you are a strong young man and a good worker.

I only know one way to work and that's not to goof off.

Where do you two know each other? asked Jack.

We belong to the same organization. We've seen each other at parties and other times, Beatrice added quickly.

(Allan nodded).

Allan, you asked me once to dance. Remember? You should remember because you held me very tight and I felt something hard.

Allan looked at the floor, flushed and nodded.

(After dinner) Thank you for dinner Jill, Beatrice. It was delicious. Reminded me of mom's cooking, said a satisfied Allan.

Jill, Jack. Let Allan and me clean up, wash the dishes, said Beatrice. It's a beautiful night. Go for a walk or a drive. I know where everything goes. Is that okay with you Allan?

Okay, I guess, said Allan a bit puzzled.

Jack and Jill picked up the cue. That's very kind of you Beatrice, Allan. I have to return a book to the library in town otherwise it will be overdue. We'll be back in one hour.

(Jack and Jill return in one hour and tiptoe into the house).

They're not in the kitchen, whispered Jack.

The kitchen is clean, whispered Jill.

(They heard some gentle moaning from the guest room. They looked at each other, went on the porch, smiled, hugged, kissed then sat on the sofa swing. Jack's arm around Jill).It's a beautiful night, darling, said Jill.

Not that it matters, I wonder what sex it will be? asked Jack.

Dr. Brown will tell us in time.

Will he deliver or will you use a mid-wife, a doula?

I'll discuss that with Dr. Brown. He's getting on in years and there are two great ones in the area.

Oh hi, Jill, Jack said a happily disheveled Beatrice. When did you get back?

Oh, we just came back this minute and the sky was so beautiful, we decided to watch it, said Jill.

Where's Allan? asked Jack.

He's in the bathroom and will be out soon.

Jill, I have to clean the van so that I can drive Allan home. Will be back in ten minutes, said Jack with an expression that Jill correctly picked up. See you in a bit.

Beatrice. You were in bed with Allan and I'm very happy for you. Did Allan know what to do?

He listened to me and it was great. I know that he enjoyed himself. And so did I. We agreed to be boy and girl friend.

That's wonderful Beatrice. Beatrice, Jack and I will be getting married on Sunday December the 15th and I want you to be my Maid Of Honour.

Oh Jill. I'm so happy for you. Yes! I will.

No special outfit. Wear what you want. You and Allan will be invited as a couple.

Hi girls. The car is ready. Where's Allan?

Here I am, said a smiling disheveled Alan.

Are you ready to go? asked Jack.

Yep!

Jack! Wait a minute, said Beatrice.

Sure, Beatrice, what's up?

Taking Jack aside: Remember a long time ago when I was crying at the jamboree and you made me feel better?

Jack nodded.

Do you remember the promise you made me?

I remember very well. I promised you that if you had a boy friend and that that you really liked each other, I would teach him a love song to sing to you if he could sing or a poem that he would recite to you. Either or both at the jam. Or you would kick me where it would hurt if I didn't. Wow! Does that mean Allan is your boyfriend?

Beatrice nodded her head vigorously and beamed.

Leave it with me. A promise is a promise and a kick where it hurts is a kick where it hurts.

You promised!

I did and I'll keep it. You just wait and see.

Hey Allan, jump in the car and we're on our way.

(While driving). Allan, you really like Beatrice, don't you?

Yep! I really do. We made love tonight. Never felt anything like that. My first time and I did everything right according to Beatrice. She even told me that I don't have to wank myself anymore now that I'm her boyfriend.

That's great Allan. Allan, do you sing or read?

Both. Why?

CHAPTER 12

WEDDING DAY

Randy we're very grateful to you for overseeing the erection of the tent, chairs, heaters. I needed an engineer's brain for that. As well, Judy and Beatrice have set up the potluck dishes—I hear that they're absolutely delicious and varied.

You bet! said Randy. As well, I've arranged the songs that you wanted the band to play—they're good guys. Seems like there are about 20+ guests.

Randy. You're not going to pull any funny stuff are you?, asked Jack.

Like what happened at our wedding? replied Randy. Oh no! Like what happened at our wedding? Like when you were sloshed out of your mind, got up on the stage and told everyone to get up from their tables because you wanted to guide them through the Macarena. The Pastor, his wife, mom, dad, my in-laws were already to go and what did you sing? Popularized by Weird Al: Fuck the Macarena. Oh no! Nothing like that, Jack. Those lyrics are burnished in my brain to this day and in all probability for life. Remember them or were you too pissed?

Here we go, here we go, hah hah hah
Sorry motherfuckers do the Macarena
Could it be that everyone's kinda gone insane, ha!
Every fucker hates the Macarena

Fuck the Macarena

Mike spit out his sax and fell to the floor in hysterics as did Marg who couldn't sing. Steve the drummer tossed his sticks away and joined Marg and Steve. The other guys in the band were laughing their guts out. Hey guys, you yelled back at them, get it together which they did. And you did the choreography with a straight face—verse after verse after verse. Audrey, stifling hysteria, with her bridal gown lifted high ran to the men's restroom to pee—there was a long line to the women's— saying hi to the guys at the urinals and entered a cubicle. By stifling my hysteria, I nearly shit in my pants. Fortunately, they were all good sports about it and decorum was re-established. Now back to the present. When Amos is ready, he will signal me, I will signal the band to start the music, you and Jill will walk hand in hand from the house, down the porch stairs into the tent—the dais will be to the right of the opening.

Thanks Randy. It's simple enough. By the way, what's the overhead for? asked Jack.

I'm going to show a retrospective of your's and Jill's life. Our mothers had almost alike picture albums as did Jill's. Jill especially will love it.

Hi Beatrice, you look gorgeous said Randy.

Thank you Randy, said a blushing but beaming Beatrice.

Beatrice, said Randy, I worked with Allan arranging the chairs, tables, electrics and dais. He's a great worker, has good organization skills and fun to work with.

I know said Beatrice with a sly smile. We do a lot of work together every day.

Then you know what I mean said Randy naively.

Hi Audrey. Jill and I are really grateful to you Randy, Beatrice and Allan for organizing all this. How's Jill, asked Jack?

She's so happy. Carol was doing the final touches to her

hair and will be ready in about five minutes. You might as well go back to the house and when you're both ready let me know, I'll signal Randy to signal Amos that you're both ready. The guests are all seated and chatting.

Thanks Audrey. I'm on my way.

Randy, You're not going to....

Yep! It will be a hoot. Pay back time!

Hi honey. You look gorgeous. I won't have any trouble consummating our marriage in the connubial bed tonight! Let's pretend that you're a virgin, that you and your mother had a mother to daughter talk the night before. Your mother advised you to tell me that you broke it when you rode a horse for the first time.

You lecher. I love you.

Hon. There's a song that is dear to me and wonder if you would like it as our bride and groom dance. I'm certain that you would be touched by the lyrics. I asked Jeff and the boys to practice it a few weeks ago. May I surprise you with it? If not, they've got a few in their repertoire than we could choose.

Jack dearest, you're always full of surprises. That's the only thing that attracts me to you. Surprise me.!

I thought that it was the way I scrub you during our sacred showers.

Jack dear, I almost forgot. I invited Dr. Brown's receptionist and her daughter Gillian who is beautiful, accomplished and available. Is there a decent guy here from your station that we could introduce to her?

Why yes! Johnny! His fiancée broke off their engagement about six months ago. Without telling Johnny that she was unhappy with their relationship, she covertly started dating a dentist. Told Johnny that she needed greater security than what a fireman could provide her. He started dating again about a month ago. He's about six feet, trim, pleasant features, a great sense of humour, responsible, emotionally and financially stable and not a skirt chaser. He'll advance career-wise. Point out Nancy and Gillian and I'll have Johnny introduce himself. Let me know when you're ready and I will signal Audrey who will start the signals.

I'm ready dearest!

Jack waves to Audrey.

(The band starts to play the bridal march). Then as Jack and Jill walk hand in hand, down the stairs to the music and as they are about to enter the tent, Randy starts to sing:

Here comes the bride,

Beaming, broad and wide,

Walking down the aisle

Wth the stud by her side.

Here comes the stud,

Who's had one too many a Bud,

With his lovely bride

Standing by his side.

(Jill smiled as did Jack who realized the game and waved his finger at Randy who waved it back). *Touché*, cuz, yelled Jack as they mounted the dais. (Then Randy and Beatrice mounted the dais. Randy and Jack hugged each other). In my dreams, I always dreamed an off-the-wall wedding.

(Just wait, cuz, said Randy to himself. Won't be as bad as the Macarena gig though).

(Amos held up his hand to silence the guests which they did slowly). Friends, guests. As many of you know, Jack has been like a son to me and Sophie and we have three daughters who are still chatting like teenage girls at a p.j. party at the back. Girls! Quiet down back there. As a Justice of Peace I am legally authorized to marry in this jurisdiction. Jack. Do you take Jill, your expectant bride, as your wife?

I do!

Jill, do you take Jack as your loving husband?

I do!

Now before I officially pronounce you husband and

wife, I understand that you want to read your vows to the guests?

(Together) Yes!

(They take out their typed sheets and read together). What we are about to read to you, dear friends, is a manifesto— essentially a living document— which we pledge to use to guide us in our life together. And build on it.

We pledge to each other that if one of us is angry with the other, to make a personal statement. i.e. "Your remark about the subject really upset me" . No name calling— "you're an idiot. No insults—"do you have shit for brains". No generalizations—"you're always doing the same stupid thing". We will not cause deep hurt to each other this way.

A murmur of oooh's were heard from the women.

We pledge to each other not to react to something one of us has done/said but to respond— the latter, to us means that we've given consideration to the other's thoughts, actions, comments. Our mothers taught us this valuable lesson years ago: "as long as it's in your mouth, you own it". To this we add: before one of us says or does anything to each other or to anyone, decide on the relationship we want to create.

More murmurs—ooohs— from the women.

We pledge to each other to resolve a heated issue that same day and not to leave issues unresolved because they will fester and worsen. Both of us will sleep better after resolving a personal issue. Makes cuddling even sweeter.

We pledge to each other that if one of us doesn't understand what was said to the other based on our response —we might be in our own thoughts which we often are and our privilege—not tot fly off the handle. We will say something to this effect: I think that you really didn't hear me properly or if you did, repeat it to me, paraphrase it back. Any misunderstandings should be rectified at that time.

Again, more murmurs from the guests both men and women.

We pledge to each other that if it's obvious that one of us is busy with something such as on a long-distance telephone call, not to barge in. Signal me or lip-speak it— how much time, when can we talk? Realizing that we need to talk, signal an estimated time with fingers/hands. If it's an emergency, barge in. In this way we will know that we are being acknowledged and not ignored.

We pledge to each other not to invalidate one another. We each will acknowledge and honour what is said to us. If we have a contrary view, we will make a personal statement. We will not let an argument degenerate. We will negotiate: a solution, a resolution in fairness via open and frank dialogue.

Murmurs, oohs mainly from the women

We pledge to each other not "mind fuck" one another. We will guard against telling one another how and what to think about a given subject. No one has any business in another person's mind— we're there by invitation only.

Oohs.

You bastard a woman at the back exclaimed unable to contain herself, then did, then looking embarrassed and apologetic for interrupting the service.

We pledge to each other that at day's end we will review the day's activities with each other and with others. If we are not satisfied with a particular aspect of it, determine how to rectify it with each other or with others. If we've done well, let's reward ourselves as fitting a husband and wife.

Not reading. Jill dear, I pledge to you before our friends that I will sit to urinate.

Yahoo yelled Amos's daughters. Hey Jack, yelled one woman, you're a leader a revolutionary. You're in the vanguard of civilized men, exclaimed another woman. Run for office and you'll surely have the women's vote. Yahoo yelled a group of women. Jack! You're selling out yelled a man—not seriously—but was shot daggers by the women. Jack waited for the comments to stop then continued.

Although your request to me, Jill dear, was, initially seismographic—it was genuinely a request, not a demand—I quickly realized that you were not trying to remake me. Women value a clean home which includes the bathroom. That you also wanted to avoid pubic hairs randomly strewn around the foot of the commode and under the commode seat is understandable.

Yukk, acclaimed some women.

And most importantly, not to have your butt feel the cold commode, or the cold water on it during a midnight visit to the loo because I forgot to lower the seat .

Right on, Jack boy!

It really makes sense, exclaimed Jack to the guests, because now when I finish my business and in a rush to go somewhere else, that dreaded you-know-what isn't roiling, rolling down my leg.

All women applauded.

Together: It's wonderful that we share the same values and are of one spiritually.

Jack and Jill fold the papers and put them away.

Well, Jack and Jill, said Amos lovingly, what you have essentially pledged to each other is a spiritual blueprint for your lives together. Spiritual means practical. Beatrice, Randy, please give the gold wedding bands to Jack and Jill. Now Jill, Jack, place them on your fingers. I now pronounce you man and wife. You may now kiss each other...... Hey! I said kiss, not start to get it on in front of the guests. Show some restraint. Then again why? May it always be, kids.

Everybody. Let's welcome the new couple, said Randy. The delicious food is ready, start lining up and sit at any table.

(Jack, Jill walk hand in hand to their table followed by Randy, Audrey, Amos, Sophie, Beatrice and Allan).

Jack, Jill, there will be some speeches about mid-way, said Randy. Then, after the meal, the first dance will be a bride and groom dance—I understand that you've chosen the song. You'll start it then I'll announce to everyone who wants, to join in.

(Mid-way.Randy stands up, taps a glass for attention). Dear guests, before you eat your desserts, I would like to say a few words about my cousin Jack. We've known each other since infancy—our mothers were fraternal twins—and we've loved each other since. We even drew closer when Jack's father abandoned them when we were kids. Jack used to discuss how important it was for him to be the man in his home and how protective he had to be of his mother. Because of Jack, we both got jobs when we were old enough, Jack to help out. We both are extremely grateful to our mothers for the values that they taught and raised us by. Life was hard but life was good. We also had fun together—we often studied together, double-dated and played on the same teams. Did you know that Jack is a fantastic, bold, creative dancer?

What's up Randy? asked Jack.

Nothing special. Guests, I've put together stills of Jack's and Jill's lives. When that's finished, something special.

(There were oohs and aahs at Jack when young. Then the women whistled at Jack when he was a lean trim teen; pictures of Jack and his mom with Randy's family at the beach; high school receiving scholarships; pictures when at college, graduation, and as a firefighter in his uniform. Then Randy showed similar pictures of Jill: a chubby little girl with pinchable cheeks and thighs, smiling, alert eyes).

Couldn't you pinch her cheeks and those thighs were some comments.

(Pictures of a chubby teen with ponytail posing with feigned attitude with her girl friends: still smiling, eyes very alert; college pictures, graduation, her first job after graduation as a landscape artist driving a dozer; the lawyer's office when she bought the farm posing with the lawyer and

Silas the farmer who sold it to her and held the mortgage with no principal payments for the first five years).

And now dear guests, something special, something rare and unique that you never will see anywhere.

(Randy slipped the DVD into his laptop. It was Jack's strip performance at the Redneck Review projected onto an overhead. Randy made a mental note of it when he learned of it at their dinner a few months ago; discovered that all performances were filmed and managed to convince the owner why he needed it of Jack only.

The guests started to clap to The Stripper, Jill and Audrey were in hysterics, some of the women who worked with Jack were standing, shouting at the overhead and started their own strip; Jack was laughing and pretended that he was sliding under the table. The three sisters rushed up to the screen and did their own dance and partial strip interacting with each other. When it was over Jack composed himself, hugged Randy and said to the guests: that's what cousins are for. To expose my shortcomings. Which drew some chuckles.

How about one now yelled a few women at the back that Jack recognized as Sophie's and Amos's daughters.

Thanks girls. I'm touched by your encouragement but from here on in the only stripping I will be doing will be of the topsoil—temporarily of course.

(Dessert and meal are finished).

Dear guests. The first dance will be a bride and groom dance then anyone can join in to honour Jack and Jill. I'll signal when you can join in.

Jack and Jill, hand in hand, walk to the centre of the dance area. The band starts to play then Jack and Jill begin….

I'll always remember,

the song they were playing,

Oh Jack dear, When I was a girl, I used to dream that Ann Murray would sing it at my wedding with me dancing and being held tightly by my prince charming.

The first time we danced and I knew
As we swayed to the music,
and held to each other,
I fell in love with you

The guests applaud. Randy takes Audrey by the hand and joins Jack and Jill, signals Amos and Sophie, Beatrice and Allan to join in, then signals everyone else.

Could I have this dance
for the rest of my life?
Could you be my partner
every night?
When we're together
it feels so right.
Could I have this dance
for the rest of my life?
I'll always remember,
that magic moment,
When I held you close to me
As we move together,
I knew forever,
your all I'll ever need.
Could I have this dance
for the rest of my life?
Could you be my partner
every night?,
When we're together
it feels so right,
Could I have this dance
for the rest of my life?

Johnny bumped purposefully into Jack. Hi Jack, Jill. Congratulations and my deepest best wishes, said Gillian and Johnny. Let me introduce you to Gillian said Johnny proudly. Gillian looked happy.

Hi Gillian, said Jack and Jill together. We're so happy that you were able to attend, said Jill.

If it works out, bring her over for dinner, whispered Jack as they hugged each other.

What did he say? whispered Gillian, after they danced away.

If it turns out that we like each other and you're okay with it, we've been invited to dinner, whispered Johnny back.

Could I have this dance
for the rest of my life?
Could you be my partner
every night?
When we're together
it feels so right,
Could I have this dance
for the rest of my life?

All guests return to their tables.

Jack stood up. Dear guests, may I have your attention. Thank you! Beatrice, please sit in this chair in front of the dais and Allan, please come up here with me. Dear guests, Allan, over here and Beatrice, over there are in love. For years they were to shy to approach each other and they finally did with a little encouragement from Jill and me.

Beatrice and Allan blushed.

Now Allan wants to sing a love song to Beatrice and I'll accompany him on guitar. This is Allan's first song ever. And in public! And to his sweetie!

Beatrice was in a mild state of shock.

Jack retrieves his guitar from under the table and tunes it.

Are you ready Allan?

Allan nervous with the mike in his hand nods. Then starts singing and looking lovingly at Beatrice then alternates with glances at the music on the music stand.

I love you, a bushel and a peck!
A bushel and a peck, and a hug around the neck!
A hug around the neck, and a barrel and a heap

A barrel and a heap, and I'm talkin' in my sleep.
About you.
About you!
About you!
My heart is leapin'!
I'm having trouble sleepin'!
'Cause I love you, a bushel and a peck
You bet your pretty neck I do!
(Jack and Allan together on the chorus:
Doodle, oodle, oodle.
Doodle, oodle, oodle.
Doodle oodle oodle oo.
I love you, a bushel and a peck
A bushel and a peck, go and beats me all to heck!
Beats me all to heck how I'll ever tend the farm
Ever tend the farm when I want to keep my
Arms - about you –
About you!
About you!
Jack and Allan:
Doodle, oodle, oodle.
Doodle, oodle, oodle.
Doodle oodle oodle oo.
The cows and chickens
are goin' to the dickens!
'Cause I love you a bushel and a peck
You bet your pretty neck I do –
Together
Doodle oodle oodle
Doodle oodle oodle
Doodle oodle oodle, oo!
Allan bows. The guests give Allan a standing ovation.
Did I do okay? whispered Allan to Jack.
Fantastic! Allan, I'll bet that you get lucky tonight and
for a bit longer, whispered Jack.

(Allan jumps down from the dais and hugs Beatrice). Allan, that was beautiful, said a teary Beatrice, as they hugged. Then gave him a kiss and the guests applauded again.

Dear guests, said Jack—Jill and I need to say a few words before we conclude. I consider myself the luckiest guy in the world for having met Jill. She even gave me a job.

The guests laughed.

Behave yourself dear or you're fired, joked Jill.

Yes, dear. As many of you know, I was despairing of ever meeting my soul mate. Now I don't know whether what I am going to say is in your respective belief systems—with some of you, I know it is—but one evening, depressed, I decided to ask the universe for her. It was about midnight on a Thursday in July last summer. I opened the window, the sky was in its full glory. I sang this song out as my prayer. It was a George Strait song that had a great impact on me and I decided to make it into a prayer, a wish a hope a dream to meet a life partner. I sang it out to the universe. I added a few of the lyrics to Before I Met You for the same reason. You're Something Special To Me.

In "D"—dog, boys. Then it will be in "G".

As I hold you close tonight
Hear what I say
There's no doubt it's love alright
'Cause I never felt this way
An angel's what you are
And now I see
You're not just some one else
You're something special to me
Every man, has a dream
And you made mine come true
How it happened, I don't know or care
I'm just happy I found you
Wrapped in the arms of love

Is where I'll be
For all the world to see
You're something special to me
It's all such a mystery
You're something special to me
"D"- Dawg.
Thought I'd stay single always be free
But that was before I met you
I said that no sweet thing could ever hold me
But that was before I met you
I thought I was swinging the world by the tail
I thought I could never be blue
I thought I'd been kissed and I thought I'd been loved
But that was before I met you
That was before I met you
Every man, has a dream
And you made mine come true
How it happened, I don't know or care
I'm just happy I found you.

Wow! Powerful! Were some comments.Then a miracle happened. Jill, will you take over?

Jill, surprised and happy, took the mike. Miracle? Friday morning, after Joanie's kids left for school, a fire broke out in her kitchen.

Joanie stands up and yells, jokingly: So that's how it happened. Jack!, it was your fault, then sits down.

Sorry Joanie, part of the ups and downs in life. Someone's misfortune is someone's fortune. In this case, we both won. You got a free bed of day lilies for your front lawn. Joanie, please come up and tell us what happened.

Joanie takes the mike. I called the fire department which came very quickly and extinguished it. Then this gorgeous Assistant Fire Chief —Jack blushes—comes over and asks in a soft spoken, gentle: Are you okay ma'am? I noticed is that he wore no ring. Ma'am, he says, I'd like to explain some basic fire prevention for the home. I invited Jack for some tea and cookies. After Jack's spiel, I sounded him out by asking him if he was dating and if he was, would he be interested in a friend?—Jill, sitting here. Expressing some doubt, he said: sure, why not. Jack?

Oh! right! I called and was skeptical. Oh! You're the fireman, Jill said—she explained that it slipped out. Usually the women want professionals, businessmen. I decided to get it over with and asked her out. Jill invited me to come up to the farm and in a short time was smitten.

Jill?I too was skeptical. But as we walked and talked, we both became aware that we were more than just attracted to each other as we shared personal experiences. Jack, should we tell them about the manure fight? said Jill.

The what? said a few.

Why not?, said Jack

As Jack and Jill told their sides: gross; yeah, yuchus. Horse manure was the glue for your relationship? Very good! Interesting! was Johnny's response with Gillian beside him holding hands and smiling..

Guys, listen. I was so taken with Jill that when she offered me a roll in the sack while standing in the stuff—she was really testing me—I refused because I respected her, was very much taken with her and wanted to get to know her better. She sure was in my thoughts that night.

The men laughed as did the women. Jill rolled her eyes.

Randy, said Jack. That's our story.Thank you all for coming and have a safe trip home.

Sophie, Amos, said Jack, I am so grateful for what you what you have done for us. Yes! We'll be at the station's Christmas party. They hug as does Jill with Sophie and they leave.

Hi Beatrice, said Jack, wasn't Allan great? We rehearsed it for about a month. At first he didn't want to—'I'm afraid that I'll screw things up', he said. Do it for Beatrice, she'll love it, I told Allan—mistakes and all. The guests are all friends, decent folk. They'll expect any beginner to goof up and will cheer you on. First we worked together memorizing the words. Then we practiced singing and pretty soon everything came together. Allan and I are becoming friends and we'll practice things from time to time. But can't promise anything definite with the baby coming.

Jack. You kept your promise. Thank you, said Beatrice with tears.

Hi Allan. Thanks for all your help. I know Randy really appreciated it.

Allan, said Beatrice, we're getting a drive back to the city. You're staying with me tonight and calling in sick Monday.

But Beatrice, I've never been sick from work.

Beatrice kisses him on the lips.

Okay, I'll call sick on Monday, with a blush and concealed ardour.

(Jack walks over to Randy to help him load the electrics into their van). Randy! Think of it! If all goes well, we'll be fathers in the Spring. Wheeling our children together in prams when we get together. They'll be cousins, close in age and close with each other.

Amen, Jack. The van is loaded. Here comes Audrey.

Audrey hugs Jack. Your virgin says that she'll be ready in her sheer negligee in a few minutes. She broke it after an accident on a boy's bike and that she's reviewing mommy's instructions. I trust that you will be up for occasion.

You women! said Jack. Love you both.

Jack dear. I'm brushing my hair and will be out in a few seconds. Please don't start without me.

END OF PART 2

PART 3

TO MAKE A
GOOD LIFE.

Kids, Family. The Real World

CHAPTER 1

(Jill gritted her teeth, straining, eyes closed tightly, gripping the rail, Jack wiping her brow with a hand towel).

Jack, if you.. ever.....oh God!.... come near me again... I'll...I'll Oh God!.. run the dozer... over you, gasped Jill through gritted teeth and grasping the rail tenaciously.

Push honey, it's almost through.

Here she is....your.....lovely....daughter. Congratulations momma and poppa. Nurse!

Quietly to the nurse: we'll probably have to do a breech extraction as per the last ultra-sound. I'll see how the little guy is positioned when I re-examine Jill.

Jack, we need to talk. The second baby will be born breech, that is feet first if I can't redirect him. It's a more risky delivery. The cord can get wrapped around his head, the shoulders could cause a problem and cause brachial plexus injuries and the like. Most of the time, the breech delivery is done via C-section if the baby is not fully engaged in the pelvic region and not too far down the birth canal. I've done many breech deliveries successfully and am willing to try the breech delivery. It will be uncomfortable and many opt for C-section.

Bottom line for me is that I want both to survive and be healthy .Let's try the breech delivery and if in your opinion C-section is required, go for it. Ok doc, proceed with the breech delivery.

Jill, I'll try to manually turn the baby while watching the ultrasound and moving him via the top of your abdomen. When I'm trying to change the position of the baby, concentrate on something to help with the pain and try not to push during each contraction. Let me know when the contractions start so that I'll stop until they stop. Jill, trying to rotate someone in your body is quite painful and I'm impressed with your courage. …..I can't turn the baby around so resume pushing…. The baby's foot is down… each contraction seems to suck her back up the birth canal….. Jill, no luck after several contractions. I'm going to wrap a piece of gauze around one foot to hold onto the baby during the contraction and to gently pull him out.

Doctor, I'm with you…..it's….. the most painful… part… Oh God!…of the delivery… for me…Oh God! … having a doctor…. with his hand inside me… holding onto my baby's… foot and pulling him out. …like what a vet… does when… delivering a colt.

Got him! Hallelujah! A beautiful boy, a healthy looking one too.

CHAPTER 2

Hi Jill, Jack. I'm nurse Meg and I'm here to discuss feeding of your twins. You did say that you were going to breast feed. Is that correct?

Yes! said Jill emphatically.

First, Jill, let's talk about you. Jack, listen good!

A mother who is nursing twins needs extra rest, extra nourishing foods, extra liquids and perhaps extra pre-natal lactating vitamins. Nursing twins requires even more daily calories. Nutritionists recommend that women nursing twins eat 3,000 calories daily. Jill, this is not the time to diet! Most women find they can eat lots of nourishing food and still gradually lose their pregnancy weight because of the calories expended by nursing two babies. Many doctors recommend that mothers who are nursing twins not try to return to their pre- pregnancy weight until the twins are at least six months old.

Although the babies should be fed on demand when possible, nursing every one to two hours is not too frequent for newborn twins. A little manipulation of feeding times may be necessary for your needs, especially if you are tandem nursing. Even if you are nursing separately, you may still want to awaken the sleeping twin and nurse him or her after nursing the first one. This will allow you to get the maximum amount of rest between feedings.

You will have to be particularly careful about preventing

sore nipples. A mother who is positioning her babies correctly on the breast in the beginning will avoid sore and cracked nipples. It is important to change nursing positions, air-dry nipples after nursing and also to maintain a good diet and get lots of rest. You need to be extra careful that your babies are latched on properly in a good nursing position.

It is unlikely that you'll be able to do more than nurse your babies and take care of herself in the first few weeks. Do not hesitate to ask Jack for specific household needs. Jack, you or hired help must take care of housecleaning, meal preparation and the like. You listening Jack?

I've already made plans, replied Jack.

Thank you dearest, said Jill.

Jack. Fathers can be quite helpful in the early days by changing diapers, bringing the babies to the mother to feed, and burping and rocking the babies. You'll bond with your babies this way. A father's support, assistance, and patience are extremely important for successful breast feeding of twins.

Now let's talk breast feeding positions. Jack, it's important that you pay attention.

I most certainly am paying attention. Imagine being able to provide sustenance to your child. I envy women their ability to do this.

Jack, you're rare! I've had only a few men over the years say that.

Back to breast feeding. Breast feeding twins simultaneously is a real time-saver. As the twins become stronger and you become more confident, tandem nursing, where babies are nursed simultaneously one on each breast, becomes easier. The twins are full-term and healthy so it is a good idea to practice tandem nursing at least once a day so both you and the twins become comfortable with it. In the beginning, you'll need help getting the twins positioned. It may be easier to position the less vigorous baby first, then put the more vigorous baby to the breast.

I'll be there to help, said Jack enthusiastically.

Experiment with different positions to see which is the most comfortable. The two nursing positions which work well for tandem nursing are the double clutch or "football hold" and the cradle/clutch. You'll have each baby tucked under an arm in the football hold like this. I'll get a chart for you when I return. Sit comfortably on a couch, bed or even the floor with lots of pillows or blankets under the babies so that you do not have to hold their weight or lean into them. Some Mothers of Twins clubs will loan a "U" shaped pillow, designed for nursing twins in this position. Jack, check them out on the internet.

If you prefer to use the cradle/clutch hold, one baby is in the cradle in breast feeding position and the second is in the football hold. This way each baby can have equal exposure to left and right visual stimulation which comes from looking up at your face, even if they have favorite sides to nurse from. You can simply alternate cradle and clutch positions. Again, I will bring you a chart.

I've loaded both of you enough. Feel free to experiment until you find a position that works for you. As long as each baby is well-positioned on the breast and they each receive equal visual stimulation, any position is acceptable. I'll be around shortly with the twins, the charts and you can start breast feeding then.

Get some shut eye, hon. I'll be sitting here when Meg returns with the babies.

Here they are, Jill. let me help you get started. Jack, elevate the bed and support Jill's back with the pillows and the blankets. Here's a pillow for the babies. The way you're sitting in bed, place the pillow across your thighs. Now here's the little girl. Place her legs to your left side, bring her to your left nipple and let her start.

Wow! She's a hungry little thing, said a pleased but still weary Jill.

Now here's the young man. Do the same but on the opposite side.

Wow again! He's hungry!

Hon, you look so beautiful nursing the babies, said Jack with tears. Forgive me for being unmanly. It's powerful. You're so beautiful. When I was in college I took an elective in Modern Art and nothing that I studied had this impact. Maybe Ruben's Cimon and Pero which electrified me was a distant second. A young Greek woman, mother of a newborn infant, sought to save her father Cimon who had been imprisoned and sentenced to death by starvation, by feeding him at her breast since she was unable to bring food past his guards.

I stared it for which seemed for hours. Honey, said Jack composing himself, would you mind my taking a digi-pic for our private album? Exactly the way you are. No makeup, hair stringy, rumpled housecoat.

I feel the way you do, dearest, said Jill. I believe that they've had enough. Jack, take your son and burp him.

CHAPTER 3

ON ARRIVING HOME

Jack, there are no cribs in the children's room?

Hon, let me explain. I bought some used cribs that are in excellent condition, but bought new mattresses. They're all in storage. Used crib mattresses often have bacterial growth giving off some kinds of toxins. Don't worry, I'll set them up when the babies are older.

We have old hardwood floors that are nailed not glued, no VOC paints for the walls which have long gassed off and I've had the house checked for geopathic stress and there's none. It's healthier for the babies to sleep with us especially you their mother. Our bedroom is totally non-allergenic as there's will be when they're ready.

Jack, we should have discussed this. Are you sure that it's safe, wise for the babies to sleep with us? I've heard, read otherwise. What happens if we roll over on the babies?

You're right, I should have discussed it with you. I never gave much thought to it until a few days ago. When I was at the Reserve reviewing the contract, the women asked me about you and I told them that you were ready to "pop". Sherry, the Chief's daughter, asked me whether the babies would sleep with us. What did I know about it? I replied that there was the assumption that we wouldn't. Who does anyway? I asked. So when Sherry began telling me of the history, benefits and advantages of us sleeping with the babies, I decided to read up on it fast. I've done quite a bit of reading on the subject and there is a plethora of misinformation. With what's going on with you and the business—don't worry, everything's on schedule— it slipped my mind. What I researched was that the modern western practice of putting babies to sleep in cribs in separate rooms is unique; in most parts of the world, babies still sleep alongside their mothers just as our ancestors did. In most Asian countries, they don't know what you mean if you ask where the baby is going to sleep. Those countries with the lowest rates of crib death, such as Japan and Hong Kong, are those where bed sharing is the norm. The physiological benefits to the baby, such as respiration regulation—the closer they are to a care-giver, the better the chance of having their breathing and body temperature regulated for them— heartbeat regulation, and temperature regulation when the baby is near her mother are well documented. As well, it makes breast feeding much easier. Rather than waiting for a baby to wake up hungry and cry, we'll be able to detect the babies squirming so that you can them feed them without either you or them having to be fully awake. So breast feeding mothers often find that they sleep better when their babies are alongside them.

How long do the babies sleep with us from your research?

According to what I've read, most parents who bed share with their infants do so for breast feeding, so some wean at three months and move babies out of bed at that time, and others continue into the 2nd year and everywhere in between. We'll have to play it by ear. For twins, the maintenance of your mother's milk supply is an important issue — that you produce enough to meet the needs of two babies. Frequent feeding and especially frequent night feeding when most prolactin is produced are crucial to maintaining copious milk production — so for us, parents of twins, bed sharing would be a helpful strategy.

Dearest, I resonate with what you've just said. What a gem you are. How can we manage two in bed dearest?

Again and according to my research, there are several methods. Some have one baby in bed at a time between mom and dad and the other in a cot by the bed, and alternate babies between these positions. I think this is most common. Others have had mom in bed alone with one baby on each side and dad elsewhere. I think this is a little more tricky as to feed one baby mom has to turn her back on the other. Another family alternated with one baby at mum's breast and the other on dad's chest, and again kept swapping them over throughout the night. Lots of parents put their twins together in the same cot next to their bed — but some have two cots, one on mum's side and one on dad's side! Whatever ways you can imagine, parents probably do it! We'll experiment what's best for us and if the opportunity arises, share it with others who have given birth to twins.

Sounds real exciting, said Jill with some uncertainty. We'll see what will work for us.

But what about during the day?

I purchased several slings so that you, even I, can wear our babies.

Baby wearing can make our lives much easier. For example, wearing baby frees yours, our hands, for basic cleaning, preparing food, running errands, and other day-to-day activities. With the babies tucked in a sling or carrier, we'll not have to stop what we're doing when the babies fuss or need reassurance. A few words, a soothing touch, and baby goes back to being contented. Leaving the house doesn't require as much preparation either. A sling or baby carrier can be folded up and stuffed into a diaper bag so that it is readily available for use. I've read that some mothers automatically put their sling on, like a jacket, whenever they head out the door.

Fascinating, dearest!

There's more, mother. We can sense when the babies are growing restless or hungry so that we could fix the situation before baby's complaints become disturbing and upsetting. The more confidence we gain, the more we can relax and enjoy them. There's more to learn but we will day by day.

Dearest, there's one little issue that has to be addressed. You're a hungry beast. I'm still somewhat attracted to you. How will we manage?

That's why cots were invented.

CHAPTER 4

Hi Randy. We were waiting for your call. Jill's fine but very tired as she had a very hard breech delivery with the second delivery—our son. She's sleeping now. It took a long time for the boy to be pulled out— like a rabbit from a magician's hat. Well, not quite. How's Audrey and your twins?

They're doing fine in fact sleeping through the night which is a relief to us and they're gaining weight as expected. They're three months old.

I can hardly wait for you and Audrey to bring them over so that they can meet their cousins. At some level there could be a connection. I know that Jill really wants you guys to come over and to have some private time with Audrey. You know! Women talk! It's very important for them.

I know. While they're having their *tete*, Jack, we can have our brew and get caught up. Changing diapers, feeding, burping, rocking them, talking and singing them to sleep, stimulating their senses. I love it. As well, I'm back in the saddle again.

Now that's what I've been waiting to hear, Randy. Congrats! We were going at it well into Jill's pregnancy. Kept the blood circulating reeaal well. She knows that I love and respect her and that we'll wait until she's totally recovered. On the other hand, with what she went through, she might not want to have sex with me ever again. If that happens,

Randy, you live in the city. Where can I buy an inflatable woman?

Don't worry, cuz! It's common. Audrey felt that way too but they'll come around on their own time.

…to God's ears, cuz.

CHAPTER 5

THREE MONTHS LATER

Honey, when are you going to resume your night out with the girls?

I never gave it a thought, dearest. We've been so involved with the twins: feeding them, changing them, carrying them around with us. I'd love to join them as they're fun and, come to think of it, I miss them.

Honey, the kids are well-fed and finally sleeping through the night. One of my fantasies when single was to rock and sing my baby to sleep while my wife was resting. Now I hold them both securely as I sing to them while rocking on the chair. Our reality is two babies and they're manageable. They've been home for three months and we're finally comfortable with them. I've stopped counting their fingers and toes several times a day a week ago.

So have I, dear.

I have a surprise for you. Carol is picking you up and driving you to her home where the girls will be. She's coming to pick you up in three hours so start prettying yourself after you've extracted your milk. Have your cell-phone on just in case the babies reject the nipples on the bottles.

Jack! You dear sweet considerate man. You make me forget that deep down you're a hungry beast. Be patient dearest. (Plants a kiss on Jack who closes his eyes savouring it).

Carol's here honey.

Dearest, there are two bottles in the fridge.

Was it difficult to extract?

Not difficult but less rewarding as two little hungry mouths weren't sucking away so contentedly.

This is a trial run. If it works, you'll be able to take more time with the girls

(At Carol's home). Jill, you look beautiful! Radiant! Motherhood suits you. You've lost some weight commented Sally with tears.

About five pounds. Jack says not to lose anymore for him. He says that Rubenesque figures are a turn on for him; "the way women are supposed to be".

Oh Jill, we're so happy for you, said Kate, with tears.

(With tears). I missed you all so much and the fun we had together since we were kids. If the babies accept the nipples, we'll be able to spend more time with each other.

What's new on the men front?

We all have beaus….

(Jack is on the rocking chair holding two babies and singing them Mother Goose Rhymes. They fall asleep and Jack places them in their cots. Cindy awakes in an hour and starts to cry as does Danny. Jack changes them).

Your bottles are warming, kids. Be back in a minute. (Jack tests the bottles on his wrist, picks up Cindy and begins to feed her. She stops sucking for a second then resumes vigorously. When finished, Jack burps her, kisses her cheek, places her in the cot and picks up a wailing Danny. Danny as well stops sucking for a second then begins sucking vigorously. Jack burps, kisses Danny's cheek and places him in his cot. Jack has two contented babies sleeping soundly and continues reading).

(At Carol's). I'm so happy for you all that you've got decent men in your lives.

CHAPTER 6

Two years later

Jack, the kids are two years of age and we parade around them in the nude. When do we cover up? They've long noticed our secondary sex characteristics.

Hon, I've often thought about it before we met and during these past few weeks. Glad that you raised the issue. You'll love this. As I was about to shave this morning, I heard Cindy and Danny playing in their room with some toys. So I'm shaving, relaxed, then I see from the corner of my eye, Cindy leading Johnny into the bathroom by his hand—both sort of waddling like typical two year olds. They both stopped between me and the vanity. They watch me shave. Then Cindy gently slaps my genitals and says "toy" then proceeds to walk out leading Danny. I couldn't stop laughing.

And neither can I, dearest.

Hon, the thought just occurred to me. Would you ever consider going to a nudist resort? There's a family, couples only facility, not more than 30 minutes away.

A what?

Yes! You heard correctly. A nudist resort.

Jack. I'm very shy about displaying my body publicly. But naked? I'll have to give the matter some thought. I should think that I would first have to lose about thirty to forty pounds so that I don't feel disgusted with myself.

Hon, don't lose one pound from your precious body. It's absolutely unnecessary. I don't want our children raised to think that human bodies are disgusting, dirty. Why would anyone want to teach that to their kids— that their bodies are dirty and disgusting? By being natural and matter-of-fact about nudity will prevent our kids from developing and harbouring an attitude of prurience or shame about the human body. I attended a family, couples only—gay or straight—nudist resort with a friend several years back and it was a delightful experience. To see children running, playing in the nude was a joy. No prurience, leering, furtive glances by these kids.

Let me think about it dearest.

Take as much time as you need, hon. If you agree, why not visit for a weekend. I can load the tent and camping gear into the van in a flash.

Let me mull it over dearest. But one thought has already occurred to me.

What's that hon?

What happens if Cindy leading Danny by the hand go around slapping men's genitalia shouting "toy"?

CHAPTER 7

TWELVE YEARS LATER.
FATHER TO SON

Hi hon, I'm home. Come out from wherever you are.

I'm on the back porch painting the old rocker.

(Jill comes in barefoot wearing an old pair of torn paint-speckled jeans and tattered silk blouse unbuttoned half way, her hair a mess slightly over her face—a turn on for Jack)

They embrace and kiss, Jack starts to gets busy. Mmm!

Jack, the kids will be home any minute, wait until tonight.

Still cain't help meself after all these years. Still get turned on when you dress like that.

Beast!

Let's put the food away. Take the meat to the freezer, I'll put the other groceries away.

We need to talk, said Jill putting away the groceries. I'll prepare some tea and let's enjoy A few quiet moments before the kids return.

Hon, the two most dreaded words a wife can say to her husband are: "We need to talk".

Jack dear. There comes a time in a father's life when he should have a father- to-son-talk with his thirteen year old son on masturbation.

(Breathing easier) On what? asked Jack feigning surprise. Actually I was procrastinating. You're right hon, it's time. But why did you broach it now?

I've noticed that Danny has started staring at the girls lately especially Cindy's friends. Probably very curious. What's more, at times his bed sheets are crusted as are some of his underpants and that's why I feel that you should have a talk with him.

You're right, hon, said Jack with a knowing familiar nod. I will. We've been open with each other over the years. Thanks for…. watching for the signs.

Why not share your teenage experiences with him? joked Jill. You're the master….never mind.

I'll give some thought to it. Hey! This is Saturday I've got to clear the weeds around our hut. I'll get him to help me and when we're finished I'll discuss it with him in the hut.

You remember doing it don't you? The story of the naughty girl who broke you in then back to your favourite pastime?

How can I forget? Anyway. My father was long gone and my mother was too shy to broach it with me. She just expected that I would, that all normal boys did it, that I was normal, so I would do it.

Have you had your mother to daughter talk with Cindy? I'd love to hear what you told her about boys and men.

We're pledged to secrecy Jack. Sorry. We've had discussions at various ages even recently on female sexuality. She's careful, discrete, adores you and will probably look for a beau in her father's image.

I can hardly wait to see my mirror image in whom she brings home, smiled Jack. She's a sensible girl—like her mother.

Where are the kids and when are they coming home?

Danny's team is playing baseball in town—he's pitching— and will bike home. Cindy is at her acrobatic dance class and she too will bike home. Both should be home shortly.

Let's start preparing lunch, said a hungry Jack. I'll set the table. What are we having?

Danny, it's the girls turn to clean up after lunch. I'll need your help to weed around the hut. An hour should do it for the both of us. What's your schedule like?

Dad, let's do it now and get over with it. I've a math test on Monday which I know that I'll ace but I don't like to get over confident so I'll need to review my notes just in case.

Thanks Danny, I really appreciated your help. Come into the hut with me. Have a seat. I've been meaning to talk to you these past few weeks. You know that I never had a father who sat me down with me when I was your age to talk about….ahh… things. About sex, ahh… masturbation. And ahh… well, you know!

Hey dad, it's okay, said Danny holding up both his hands. They teach the boys that stuff in the Sex Education classes and I sort of know all about it.

Danny, don't rob me of having a father to son talk. I have no intention of pulling rank on you as we raised you and Cindy by Adlerian methods.

Okay dad, do your fatherly thing and I promise you that I'll listen and hear you. As parents you taught us the distinction between listening and hearing and how to really listen to hear. Actually, none of my guys have had their dads talk to them.

Danny, your at the age where you'll be dating young women who are already sexually active. As you might very well be, son.

No dad, I haven't been.

Danny, my expectation of you is not to engage in promiscuous, indiscriminate sex as the opportunities will be many because you're a bright, handsome young man. In my way of thinking, intimacy, sexuality means responsibility, ethics. What does that mean to you, son?

Dad, the last thing that I want is to get a girl pregnant.

Good! Go on!

Oh! Contraception. Well, I'll wear a condom.

Good! But what happens if the condom slips off? What happens when you're so excited and believe me you will, that you can't think and you say to hell with it and hope that she doesn't get pregnant? Consider these: Is she on birth control? Prevention! Prevention! Will you try to penetrate her immediately or will you do foreplay until she is ready for you?

What's foreplay dad?

Being tender, hugging, kissing, maybe joking a bit before it really gets intense. Touching, stroking each other, learning what pleases her—not all women are the same— enjoy each other. Tell her what pleases you. She might reciprocate. There are some books in my library which you'll want to read. They have diagrams, charts. Read some and let's talk about it. You know something, I might learn something too. I'm not an expert but you get the idea. Don't use her as a masturbatory device.... masturbating in her vagina. Make certain that you like and respect her as a person and not to treat her as an object. That you're both open and clear with each other about your intentions. Now there are both men and women with whom casual sex is fine—I'm not concerned about them. My expectations of you are not to indulge in casual or indiscriminate sex—at any age— and believe me it will challenge you. You're at the age now and probably undressing the girls mentally and masturbating or starting to just as I was, did at your age. I did and it was a *tour de force* keeping my tongue from hanging out when around the girls. They knew all about male hormones well before the boys knew what they were. The toss of their hair, their giggles, those young shapely figures shimmering when they walked . Mmm! Mmm! Brings back memories as it really wasn't that long ago. I would simply go into the bathroom and, bluntly, wack off. What a relief being able to get back to my studies.

Really! (Danny laughs awkwardly).

Sometimes twice a day especially on weekends. My mother knew what I was doing but never talked to me about it. She expected me to, that it was normal for boys. Married men and women do it. I do it. Mother does it as well.

You and mom do it? Dad, you and mom have a great sex life.

(How the hell does he know? said Jack to himself). Yes we do, but how do you know?

Occasionally, I get up late at night to go to the bathroom and I hear you and mom going at it. I don't mean to embarrass you any more than you' are now, dad, but it's music to me knowing that my parents still love and enjoy sex with each other. I don't hear the other guys talking about their folks. But you have such a great sex life, why do you "abuse" yourself?

Danny, there are times when I have a strong need, urge if you will, to be intimate with your mother and if she's too tired, I'll "abuse" myself —like a school boy. Or, mom just might lend me…. a helping hand.

Really? Mom's sexy like that?

Believe it, son! There are times when I'm at a business meeting or whatever, there are single women who could rewrite the book on coquetry—they know all the tricks. I can feel my blood being diverted to my nether regions. I love your mother dearly and adultery is not on my radar. I'll come home and resolve the matter with your mother. Resolve the matter with your mother. And I'm certain it's the same with her. Fantasize, yes! Adultery, never! There are times when I come home bagged and mom wants to get it on and all that I want to do is shower and hit the sack. Yes! We do have a great loving relationship which translates into a great sex life and hope that when you find your soul mate, with the help of your sister—listen to her, she's developing into a wise woman—you'll have a similar relationship.

Getting back to everyday matters with a tip from an old pro. Rub some olive oil on your hands as it will really enhance the session. Funny that this thought popped into my mind. I read Philip Roth's Portnoy's Complaint years ago when I was a teenager and if I remember correctly he had a chapter titled Wacking Off and it was either in that chapter or somewhere in the book that he got it off with liver that his mother bought. All the guys who read the book tried it with liver and wow! We joked about it for weeks. Thanks for listening to me son. It wasn't as embarrassing as I thought it would be.

Thanks for sharing, joked Danny. Actually, I appreciated it.

Son, it's normal and healthy. If you don't do it you'll have a wet dream. Nature will do it for you.

Have you ever had one dad?

Oh sure! Women have them as well.

They do?

Yes but let's get back to my wet dreams. Several during my teen years. Never knew what it was until the first one happened. Nobody was around to explain the phenomena. When I was a teenager, I worked on a farm one summer and bunked with three other guys and we were all strangers. At the outset, one of the boys, who fancied himself as the leader, offered a challenge as to who could hold out the longest without wacking off. "I dunno" was our response as we looked sheepishly at one another. I think that it was after a month that I had the sweetest lucid dream. I dreamed that I saw Lynda Carter, Wonder Woman, climbing out of a swimming pool in a white bikini, her long sexy hair dark and wet. Then it started, like a Victoria Day Roman candle in slow motion! What the hell! I said to myself as I woke up. What a mess! Cleaned myself as best as I could and went back to sleep. I told them what happened and as far as I was concerned, the endurance contest was over.

That's a funny story, dad. I had one recently too. Messy but the sweetest of dreams as well. Very lucid too.

Aren't they! Amazing!.

I love you dad.

I love you, son. (They hug). Now let's see how the girls are doing.

CHAPTER 8

The men will be home in about half an hour and it's our turn to prepare dinner, dear. How about if I prepare the salad, dressing and the veggies and you prepare a meat dish?

Mother, I need your advice. The school year has just started and whenever Pat and I walk past a gang of these boys who are loitering they all start making these awful comments. Like barking dogs on an imaginary leash. They are big boys, over six feet tall. We simply ignore them. Should we tell them where to go?

Dear, I suggest that you continue your conversation with Pat and don't show them that you've reacted to their taunts. I know that it's awful, scary when these immature juveniles taunt you. Don't ever let them see that they've gotten to you. If they really become bothersome, talk with Danny. As you know like his father, he's on the boxing, wrestling teams, made the district all-star football team. And not a stranger to brawling when necessary. When he walks with you and if he hears any taunts I'm certain that he'll address the boys.

Thanks mom. Only as a last resort. I have my period and liver smells good to me, saw some in the fridge yesterday. I'll prepare a special recipe that I've just found.

Mom, there's only about a quarter pound remaining. I thought that I saw a few pounds a few days ago.

I'm puzzled as well, dear. Oh, here come the men. I'll ask your father.

Here's my hard working men, you deserve a hug and a kiss. Mmmm! Now here's your hug, Danny.

Danny and I had a hard day but we overcame the adversity. Didn't we Danny?

Sure did dad!

Dear. Perhaps you can clear up this mystery. We had a few pounds of liver a few days ago and now there's hardly any remaining.

Dad, please excuse me. I just remembered the solution to that advanced math question my teacher assigned me. Be back to join you all soon.

Jack, Do you know what happened to the liver?

Why no!, said Jack fearing that his nose would grow six inches.

Well, actually yes. Let's talk in private.

You and your son, it's obvious that he has inherited certain of your genetic propensities, said Jill lovingly and with wit. He'll be a beast, just like his father. Why don't we all go out for dinner and celebrate your overcoming adversity? I'll make up a face-saving story about the liver.

Hey kids, dad's springing for dinner so be ready in 10 minutes.

Where are we going, Dad? asked Cindy.

Sweetie, there's a new restaurant in Mule Kick everyone's talking about.

What's its name? asked Danny who solved the advanced math problem in quick time?

Crudite'.

Oh, it sounds fascinating. I've been thinking about a raw food diet for some time, said Cindy.

Sweetie, it's none of the above. It opened a few months ago and people go there to be insulted by these rude, crabby old men who are the waiters. And they're hilarious. Just don't take anything they say as personal or to heart. They're there to insult, humiliate and mock in between courses but leave you alone to enjoy the food which is sort of French and pretty good I hear.

So how many are you? asked the maitre de impatiently drumming his fingers on the lectern.

There are four of us said Jack. (All four are now primed for the insults, putdowns).

Follow me. Here's your table. Sit!

(They all sit)

If I order a steak, how long will it take?

Are you getting impatient already? Hold your horses. Sumethin' wrong with you?

No! Nothing, I'm just curious.

About 20 minutes, maybe 25.

Do you have a magazine or paper that we could read while waiting?

Look shmuck, this is a restaurant not a lending library.

(Jack stifles a laugh with a smirk, Jill doubles over laughing. Danny and Cindy give each other a knowing look that this will be a different dining experience).

Sorry that I asked.

You should be sonny. Now whaddya all want?

Jill? asks Jack.

Hmm, lets see. The lamb chops. Are they good?

Look lady, if they weren't would they be on the menu? We don't serve dreck here.

That's comforting, said Jill with a smile.

That's what I'm here for.

I'll have the lamb chops, baked potatoes, and your garlic asparagus.

Wonderful! And for dessert?

For dessert I'll have your delicious New York style blueberry cheese cake.

Look lady, with your ass, you should skip dessert or have a fruit cup.

This broke Jill into hysterics. Okay, I'll take your advice and skip dessert. Thank you for your concern.

That's what I'm here for.

I'll have the same, said Jack (wincing in anticipation).

I thought so. Another man who can't make up his own mind. Order what a real man orders.

You're right. I'll have your quiche special. (Saying "duck" to himself and wincing)

Oh I never would have guessed (with an effeminate wave of the hand). Mr. Brokeback Mountain, Mr. Homo on The Range.

My name's Jack, said with a smile. (Jill is in hysterics. The kids are laughing, bellies heaving, faces hidden by menus).

Yah right!

Okay kids name your poison, the young dyke first.

Cindy going along with it). I'll have the fried liver and onion special.

Look butch, with those zits, maybe you should have it grilled instead of fried?

(Laughing). I guess you're right and you don't need to tell me "that's what you're here for". All the girls are having their hair cut Ellen DeGeneres for the summer and wearing "fuck me boots.

(The waiter with a twinkle in his eye). Aha! A lady of the night as well. Never served a family of freaks like you people before. Is this young wanker next to you one of your tricks, butch?

(Jack and Jill have their faces buried in the menus laughing and looking at each other)

As a matter of fact he is. We're breaking him in tonight, said Cindy in a casual way with straight face.

(Danny buries his head in the menu starts to slide under the table trying to restrain himself).

Good. Fatten him up before the slaughter. And whaddya want junior?

(Getting a hold of himself) I'm afraid to ask, let me see.

Go ahead, I'm here to help.

Yah right! I know. I know.

Make up your mind junior, I don't have all night. Do you see those hungry faces sitting at those tables waiting to be served? The cheapskates over there won't leave me their usual farckuckteh tips if I keep them waiting one farckuckteh minute longer.

I'll try your cheeseburger with a chef salad.

Whaddya mean try? You take a bite then you decide maybe?

You're right, I should have been more precise. Thank you.

That's what I'm here for.

I know already! I'll order the cheeseburger with a chef salad, dressing on the side please.

He's such a polite boy for a wanker you've got here butch. Treat him well.

I promise that I will. That's what I'm here for.

Very good!

(On the way home and still laughing)

I would have throttled him years ago for his remark about my fat ass.

Homo on the range. That's a new one.

My sister the dyke. Haw haw.

My brother the wanker. Haw haw and another haw for good luck.

Okay sis, you win this one, laughing.

Dearest, kids, we should go there monthly to celebrate birthdays and other special occasions. The waiters will keep us humble.

CHAPTER 9

Hi Honey, I'm ho.. Oops. Didn't realize that you're on the phone.

Hold the line, Joanie. Dearest, I'm on the telephone with Joanie, how'd it go?

We got paid in full for the mall project, deposited it in the bank. Continue your conversation with Joanie.

Where was I Joanie. Right!.

Jack straddles Jill's legs and starts to unbutton her blouse and nibble her neck. Jill starts to suppress a giggle. "So what did she do? asked

Jill.

Now Jack pulls her blouse over her shoulders then starts to unfasten her bra.

I didn't hear that clearly, Joanie, would you mind repeating it, suppressing a giggle. Oh, Jack's back and has started to become amorous. Call you back.

Hon, the kids won't be home tonight as they're on sleepovers, whispered Jack. There's plenty of hot water

Beast! What's in the brown bag?

A new domestic wine that Wal Mart is carrying called White TrashFindel.

Oh lovely, sarcastically. You expect to wine and bed me with such an elegant sounding wine?

You betchum! Now with your okay, I'd like to go to the Redneck Review at Mule Kick where they've got an "open-mike" format—first time there— and I hear it's going to be exciting, hilarious. And, I've got a routine to perform.

What's it all about?

You'll find out soon enough.

White Trash Findel, Redneck Review? Wine and bed me. Secret routine? Kids gone for the weekend. Anything else you got in mind beast?

Are you game?

Have I ever not been?

CHAPTER 10

AT THE REDNECK REVIEW

Hey everyone, wasn't Patsy great? Never knew that we had such talent in the area. Let's hear it for the producers who brought the open-mike venue to Mule Kick, tell them that we want them back once a month. (Wild applause).

Folks, we've got a newcomer to our open-mike coming up next—first time ever on the circuit. People, when it's open-mike you can expect anything. Put your hands together forrr… Jack. Hey Jack, come on up. Whatcha got for us?

Thanks Bill. There's been something brewing on my mind for years. Now before we go home all chuckled up, there's a philosophic issue near and dear to me and presumably you guys out there as well. What's this? you begin asking yourself, to the person next to and behind you. Philosophy shit at this circus? Let me explain. Several years ago, the Vagina Monologues—yah, you heard me: V- A-G- I- N- A- if you didn't catch it and if you Golden Agers didn't have your hearing aids cranked up, was a poignant and hilarious tour of the last frontier, the ultimate forbidden zone. The Vag Dialogues was a celebration of female sexuality in all its complexity and mystery for women. Oh sure! we guys got dragged to the performances—if we didn't go we'd not enjoy the subject matter for ages. As well, it was a clarion call to end violence against women. The Monologues gave voice

168

to women's deepest fantasies and fears, guaranteeing that no thinking, decent male who reads, watches it performed, will ever look at a woman's body, or think of sex, in quite the same way again. It is witty and irreverent, compassionate and wise. So! it's at this juncture I introduce to the world the Dick Monologues.

Yea and go for it came from the males in the crowd.

Hey guys, it might not be what you think. Instead of the typical fatuous stories around "dicks" and "dick heads", I will monologue about how a guy can do his part in developing a positive relationship with his woman so as not to be a "dick head"— not that I expect a woman to assume a passive role either. But first an obligatory "dick" joke—an "oldie", I can't be totally original— which I hope won't be contrary to your version of Genesis—must have been edited out at the final draft.

.. And God appeared before Adam and said: Adam. IIII've got goooood news and IIII've got baaaad news for you.

What's the good news, my Lord?

The goood news, Adam, is that I've given you a brain and a dick.

Then what's the bad news, my Lord.

Adam. The baaad news is that there's not enough blood to run them both together.

And that's problem with a lot of us guys. We should be using our brains before we use our dicks, or the corollary: we can't use our brains when we're using our dicks. Hey guys, I've been there, believe me (holding up his hand in attestation).

Many years ago I wrote an essay titled forget about the movie how to lose a guy in ten days, concentrate on staying together for life in 10 days. In the movie, Kate knows that Mathew will act like your typical "dick head" by placing feminine hygiene products in the medicine chest and hanging washed panty hose over the shower bar and the like. My God, I said to myself. That's me as well! So I decided to write an essay to myself originally titled How Not To Be a Dick Head which turned out to be Part 1 of my essay—essentially to honour, respect and enjoy those characteristics that are uniquely feminine. When I finished I asked myself: is that it in relationships? Well hardly! After I completed it, I felt that there were other issues in inter-personal relationships which are Parts 2&3. I'll read Parts 1 & 2 from my cards as soon as I locate them. They're here somewhere.

Fundamentally, your woman needs to know that she's cherished, appreciated and men, in our own way, need it as well. Although we may be complete as individuals when we meet, we need each other in order to grow into the people we need to be for that relationship. Provide the correct environment and it'll soar. Ah! Found the cards. Here it goes, not that I got it right early on, but I did make an earnest effort:

When I drive you to work in the AM, I'd love it if you'd apply your make-up in the car and not at home—if not all the time, then some of the time—it's delightfully and excitingly feminine. If we live together, may I watch you apply your makeup? If I catch you watching me shave from the corner of my eye, I'll flex my biceps. Remember this: male hormones are strongest in the AM.

Wash and hang your panty hose and panties over the shower bar. It's delightfully and excitingly feminine.

Make certain that you leave a huge supply of feminine hygiene products—napkins, tampons, liners and the like—in the medicine chest. A constant reminder, not that I need one but fun non-the-less, that I'm living with a woman. Leave a bit of room for my shaving brush and razor.

Use my razor on your legs and pits. I'll love it when I scrape my whiskers with a dull blade. It means that its time to change the blade. I know that you want to be presentable to me and especially to other women.

If you find that you've gained ten pounds or so, please consider coming to me and crying about it —I'll love it. I will tell you to gain 10 more pounds, that it wont make any difference to me, that there's more to grab, that women have to be fat— in the right places of course. I'll mean it.

And when that time of month arrives, to a typical guy who doesn't watch the calendar, leave me a little "memento" such as maybe like a little wrapped package on perhaps the washroom basin. In this way I can prepare myself for the moment when you can't suppress the urge to hacking me to pieces with your machete. Remember that I'm reasonably sensible with a good sense of humour. Although I may lose my bearings from time to time, I am committed to our relationship.

I realize that it's not that I've done any wrong. It's just that I happen to be there: perhaps enjoying a beer and watching a sporting event; or even at my work bench singing merrily away; reading quietly while in a state of male relaxation on the sofa with a glass of wine or even snoozing there. I realize that my simple , uncomplicated, quiet contented male self can tip the scale.

Take as long as you need to get dressed for a party. I know that a woman feels more like woman when she finally decides on the appropriate outfit reflecting the mood of the occasion, the accessories, the hair—am I omitting anything?— before going out the door. I will be nearby with a magazine and happy to offer a male's opinion—for all that it's worth— on the work-in-progress.

As well, when buying clothes, take me into the fitting room—lots of fun. Keeps the sales women wondering what's with the giggling.

When you first introduce me your friends say at a party or at subsequent affairs, I feel flattered when you put your arm in mine and promenade us all over. I love being "scent-marked".

It's important for you to maintain your friendship with your girl friends—don't forsake them just because we're together. Make certain that you have your girls' night out as frequently as practical. Then I can have my boys night out—you know them all as decent, fun-loving, caring and supportive. It's okay with me if you are still friends with a former husband, boyfriend with whom things didn't quite work and is a decent guy. I'm the one living with you and have the confidence in knowing that we love each other.

Guys, if you can manage this part, I feel that you're on your way. Part 2 really is how to have fun with each other. Here's how I wrote it and we're here tonight as part of our weekend.

Give an obscene phone call. Really lay into it with deep breathing and your choicest of word pictures. However, a word of caution: before you launch into it, make certain that she/he is at their work station to receive the call to avoid this kind of situation: "why Jack, I never knew that you felt that way about me". "Sorry fella, I thought Jill was at her desk".

Every now and then have a "dirty" weekend. Call me from work and make a date. Take me to a restaurant, order a cheap bottle of wine and go to say a strip show or even an open-mike show afterwards. Tell me that if I'm a good boy/girl and behave myself, I might get lucky—I don't mean at the casino's black jack tables. Make out in the back seat? Well, if we're both are still spry, agile….

If either one of us is entertaining a business associate at home, and the other brings out tea and snacks, whisper in my ear that you want to get it on tonight even if you're not up to it. We'll try not to blush or smirk.

If you're having a telephone conversation with your girl friend, I just might start unbuttoning your blouse, undoing your bra and start making out with you. You might try something similar with me. You know where to start.

Multi-form and manifold are the ways you can have fun with each other. You get the idea.

The complete text of Parts 3, which is psych oriented and a bit heavy for this format, were our marriage vows that we pledged to each other which will be posted on my blog on Wednesday as I believe that I've been on a bit too long. Feel free to comment, add to the Dick monologues—anonymously or otherwise—so that we have something to share. No gratuitous obscenities or profanities please.

(Putting the cards away).

A woman from the audience. "Hey Jack, read us your marriage vows". (More shouts from women) Please Jack, we're interested.

(Jack, pointing to his watch, looking at Bill who nods).

"Thanks, girls, I appreciate your asking".(Retrieving his cards and locating the one with their vows). Here goes. As mentioned, we read these together to our guests:

We pledge to each other that if one of us is angry with the other, to make a personal statement. i.e. "Your remark about the subject really upset me" . No name calling—"you're an idiot", no insults—"do you have shit for brains"?, no generalizations—"you're always doing the same stupid thing". We will not cause deep hurt to each other this way.

We pledge to each other not to react to something one of us has done/said but to respond— the latter, to us means that we've given consideration to the other's thoughts, actions, comments. (Jill) My dear mother always cautioned me when I was a kid: "as long as it's in your mouth, you own it". To this I add, before one of us says or does anything, decide on the relationship we want to create.

We pledge to each other to resolve a heated issue that same day and not to leave issues unresolved because they will fester and worsen. Both of us will sleep better after resolving a personal issue. Makes cuddling even sweeter.

We pledge to each other that if one of us doesn't understand what was said to the other based on our response —we might be in our own thoughts which we often are and our privilege—not tot fly off the handle. We will say something to this effect: I think that you really didn't hear me properly or if you did, repeat it to me, paraphrase it back. Any misunderstandings should be rectified at that time.

(Jack sensed a palpable silence)

We pledge to each other that if it's obvious that one of us is busy with something such as on a long-distance telephone call, not to barge in. Signal me or lip-speak it— how much time, when can we talk? Realizing that we need to talk, signal an estimated time with fingers/hands. If it's an emergency, barge in. In this way we will know that we are being acknowledged and not ignored.

We pledge to each other not to invalidate one another. We each will acknowledge and honour what is said to us. If we have a contrary view, we will make a personal statement. We will not let an argument degenerate. We will negotiate: a solution, a resolution in fairness via open and frank dialogue.

We pledge to each other not "mind fuck" one another. We will guard against telling one another how and what to think about a given subject. No one has any business in another person's mind— we're there by invitation only.

We pledge to each other that at day's end we will review the day's activities with each other and with others. If we are not satisfied with a particular aspect of it, determine how to rectify it with each other or with others. If we've done well, let's reward ourselves as fitting a husband and wife.

Now you women out there might find this pledge amusing: I pledge that I would sit to urinate. Now guys, you might think that I've sold out. But think about it!

Bravo yelled most of the women.

"Bill, allow me a few more minutes".

The audience shouted encouragement, Bill smiled and nodded)

Now into the lighter aspects of dickery, I offer you a personal experience that could be, not sure as yet, an integral part of the Dick Monologues to be shared with the world. Now where can I begin with this *geschichte*, this story, this monologue. But before I do, I'm throwing this out to the guys. Guys, especially you older guys or those recently bounced out of a relationship: what's your greatest fear? Anybody? That's right in the third row—what I call the Dead Dick Syndrome. Now if is anyone brave enough to admit it, raise your hand. No, actua…(being interrupted)

Hey Jackie boy, yer hand isn't raised. You've raised the issue, it must have happened to you.

Actually, friend, before you interrupted, I was going to say that it would be too much, too painful, too embarrassing for a guy to admit in public—women usually don't have that issue. And yes! It did happen once, in first year college. 'Twas the night before an English Grammar exam. I knew my stuff and decided to spend the evening with my then girl friend at her apartment. We're getting it on good and at the moment of truth…. dangling participle? shot through my head.

"What turned you off me dear? she asked sympathetically and of course hurt. Oh! I said as I slowly rolled over on my back with my fingers massaging my eyebrows and offering her the predictable male re-assurance: It'sss… not you Peggy. I've got the exam on my mind.

Can we talk about it dear?

Folks, I'll leave you here. Please give some thought to my suggestion. Thanks for listening and I hope that the producers of the show will be back in Mule Kick next month for an open-mike. Have a safe trip home.

There was a palpable silence, then an appreciative applause

Let's hear it forrr.....Jack. Hope to see you folks next month. With the talent you've seen tonight, I'm sure that we'll be back. Jack, whispered Bill, what the fuck is a dangling participle?

Give me five minutes, Bill, got to take a loo break and find Jill.

Jack dearest. How funny, profound, daring. So that's what you were rehearsing in your spare time and why you bought that full-length standing mirror that you have in the basement.

Honey, I hope that I didn't come across crude because anything with the topic of a dick would lead someone to think it to be that way. I wanted it to be educational, ethical and light-hearted, to challenge others to add their own experiences to it anonymously, or whatever and who knows: a road show? but not for me. And, why not the Dick monologues, Chapter 1?

CHAPTER 11

A FEW YEARS LATER

Enjoy yourselves at the prom kids. Who'll be driving?

We decided, said Cindy, that I'll drive there and Danny will drive home.

Enjoy yourselves said Jack and Jill in unison standing together with their arms around each others waist.

They're growing up so fast, said Jill with a tear as they walked back into the house.

Yes! Both handsome and intelligent said Jack, easing himself onto the sofa and pulling Jill down beside him.

Remember how carefree we were before they were born, said Jill. Now we worry about them from the time they arise in the morn and until they're in bed at night.

And it won't change even when were old and gray, replied Jack. I wouldn't have wanted it any other way. Our lives have been blessed. Remember when we first laid eyes upon each other? I tried not to be skeptical, judgmental, pleading with myself on the drive up. I looked into your eyes and they were alive. Your smile welcomed me—a sign for the direction our relationship was to take for those first 10 days. Then when we walked and shared our lives I knew that I finally met my soul mate.

Good thing that you didn't look at my ass and grimace otherwise you would have been toast. Oh sure, you were handsome and I asked myself what's he want with a fatty like me. But, I too kept an open mind and when you opened up to me I knew that you were serious. Then I became serious.

Then we both became serious. There's lot's of hot water left and the kids won't be home for several hours.

Beast!

CHAPTER 12

Cindy, there are so many girls here I don't know which one to ask to dance. What about that blonde over there?

Junior, with her hooters in the next time zone, she's trolling for guys with no appreciation for subtlety or imagination. She's not for you.

Shit! I respect your judgment but I can't my eyes off her boobs.

Then work it out when you get home, junior. Get focused.

What about that redhead over there?

Let me see. Hmm. No! She's got bitch written all over her.

Really? How do you women know these things?

Someone has to keep you males on the straight and narrow. Now see that brunette over there with the glasses. I take some classes with her. She's bright, intelligent, decent and in my acrobatic dance class. Got a nice figure which she doesn't flaunt. As an ass man, you'll like her.

What do you mean an ass man?

Come on junior. I watch you when the girls go by and the laser trail that your eyes leave is obvious as to what's your pleasure.

I like faces too, in case you haven't noticed.

I have. Now go over and introduce yourself before someone beats you to it.

Okay sis. Wish me luck.

Hi, May I sit down? My name is Danny.

You certainly may. You didn't have to introduce yourself because I know Cindy. But I appreciate your asking.

Is this your first year here? asked Danny

No, I started the same year as you.

Strange that our paths haven't crossed all these years.

They have now. Are you involved in any extra-curricular activities?

Only gym and track. I wanted to concentrate on my studies in my final year. Otherwise it was the usual for boys in the early years: football, boxing, wresting and of course, the debating society. But what about you?

Similar but I just restrict it to acrobatic dancing classes along with Cindy.

Cindy loves it. I remember a routine she proudly showed us at home when she was eight. We pushed all living room furniture to the wall and wow! We were so proud of her. And Cindy, happy, felt so accomplished to be able to perform for her family.

Your family seems to be a warm, close family, said Jill.

It is! Cindy and I realized way back that we were blessed to have such a warm and loving home.

The d.j's voice announces: "now here's an oldie but goodie. A romantic number that our parents even grandparents danced to. Johhny Mathis aaaannndd his.... Chances Are"

Would you like to dance?

I'd love to.

(Dancing about six inches apart).

By the way. What's your name?

Alice.

Hi Alice. I'm Danny.

Pleased to make your acquaintance, Mr. Danny.

Pleased to meet your acquaintance, Missy Alice.

What part of the gym classes do you like best, Danny?

I like the tramp and mat work. You?

Nothing in particular. I just like to keep fit. Do you play any musical instruments? asked Alice

Hey, great that you asked. My dad and I "noodle" at guitar together and we try to sing as well—country, western, Dylan, you name it. We're working on "Rocky Top". In a manner of speaking, he sort of proposed to my mom by guitar and song at the jamboree years ago.

Really? It sounds so romantic.

Yeah! They're a great couple. Their courtship was story-book like. Still affectionate and playful with each other. Do you play, sing, knit. quilt and the like?

My parents gave me piano and voice since I was a kid. Dad plays the fiddle and mom, banjo, so we have our own little jams. And of course, mom and I quilt along with other women. Do you quilt Danny?

You're funny, Alice. Why haven't I seen you around?

Perhaps you were looking in another direction when I happened to be nearby.

Alice, what are your plans after graduation?

I intend to study music and voice, then to teach. Mom teaches music.

And you Danny?

My mom is a landscape architect and owns Jill's Landscape Architecture. I love working with the land, the earth. Dad, who's an Honour English grad and works with mom, suggests that I get a good all-round education before deciding on a major. And most of all I love working with my dad and Cindy. I'll decide soon. They'll support whatever decision I make. I might take up quilting but not promising myself though.

You're funny Danny. It's also well-known in school circles that you're an honour student and shouldn't have any difficulty getting into any of the colleges.

(She presses her body against Danny's and when her soft-scented hair brushed his face and cheek he stopped and his body stiffened and slightly shuddered for about five seconds).

Are you okay?

Alice, please excuse me for a few minutes. Please, please don't go away.

(As he walks quickly to the boy's washroom Cindy asks: what's going on?)

Tell you later.

(Danny cleans himself in the washroom and composes himself). Shit! Shit! Shit! How the hell did that happen? smacking his fist on the vanity. Good thing that I wore my jock strap. I thought that I had more self control. I hope that Alice didn't realize what happened and that she's still waiting. Here goes.

Hi Alice, thanks for waiting. I must have eaten something that I was allergic to.

Would you like to tell me about it? suppressing a smile.

Oh, it could have been one of several foods.

Danny, would you like to go outside where the air is fresh? It could help to dissipate an allergic response.

I'd love to Alice.

(On the way home)

Cindy. She's bright, beautiful, a subtle sense of humour and understanding. So different.

I know but what do you mean by understanding?

Sis. I don't know how or why but when she pressed her body against mine when we were dancing, it was beautiful. At the same time when her soft-scented hair brushed my face and cheek, I came in my pants. I thought that I had more control.

You what?(laughing). Junior, the only decent thing for you to do now is to marry her. Go to her father and ask for her hand.

Oh come on sis. It was embarrassing enough. I told her that I had an allergic reaction.

Right! Women can sense these things—we're not fools—and I have great respect for Alice the way she dealt with it. Some creepy girls would have run away giggling. I'll enjoy her as a sister-in-law. Go for it junior.

I will, sis. Thanks for being there for me.

CHAPTER 13

SEVERAL YEARS LATER

Danny, do you take Alice as your wife?
I do!
Alice, do you take Danny as your husband.
I do.

Hi Alice, I don't know whether you remember me but we danced and talked at the prom last week?

Of course I remember you Danny. I enjoyed dancing and talking with you. You want to go into either agriculture or landscape architecture if I remember correctly.

You do. I decided to enter landscape architecture. My sister and I both love the land and we love working with each other and with our folks. Alice, what are your plans?

I plan on studying music at college—piano and voice. You had mentioned that both you and your dad played together.

As a matter of fact I do. I've been practicing fiddle, dad plays guitar and we jam mainly country, blue grass and some gospel. We've got Rocky Top just right. I had mentioned that dad proposed to mom at the jamboree by singing George Strait's Your Something Special to Me. Mom was so surprised. Their romance could be made into a movie as it was hilarious with spiritual overtones?

How sweet! Spiritual overtones? My interest is piqued. Spiritual? How so?

I'll try to make a long beautiful story short. Dad was 32 and despairing of ever meeting his soul mate. Then one night, mid-night, the sky was in its full glory, he opened the window and sang out a prayer asking the universe to send him his soul mate. The next morning a fire broke out in Joanie's kitchen— mom's friend in the city. Dad was Assistant Fire-Chief and spoke to Joanie who noticed that he was single and wanted to know if he would accept a blind date——with mom. And in ten days, they decided to live together and marry several months later.

Wow Danny. Very warm and touching story.

How did your parents meet?

They were sweethearts since high school and married after they graduated from college. They had such little money when they started. Dad just got his first job as an engineer and mom, as a music teacher. They scrimped and saved like many young couples at the time. After dad felt confident enough, he started his own firm and became successful enough so that mom could be a stay at home mom.

I wonder why are paths never crossed in all our years. Alice?

They have now Danny.

Alice, if you're not busy this Saturday would you like to go for a bike ride but if you are busy, perhaps some other time?

I'm not busy this Saturday and I'd love to go bike riding with you Danny. I love bike riding.

What time should I come by?

Call me about 8:30AM so that we can check the weather together and if there's no rain, bike over.

Great Alice, I'll call you Saturday 8:30AM sharp.

Hi Cindy, Thanks for the fix up, said Alice.

I went to the prom with Danny to make certain that he meet you. How'd it go?

He's sweet, bright, sensible and communicative. I felt very much at ease and comfortable with him. That he's gorgeous hasn't been lost on me either.

Yes, he's very open and communicative for a male.

I wish that I had a sister so that we could sit on our beds and discuss boys and the world in general. Even a brother. Mom had a rheumatic heart and was lucky to even have had me. Cindy. Did Danny really come in his pants?

Yes he did. He always assured me that he had self-control and he had even masturbated before going. What did you do to my poor brother? (giggling) You brushed his face with your hair. I love it!

I simply waned to be close to him, our bodies touching. My hair just got in the way.(Giggling).How do you know he… masturbated?

He told me so, doesn't want to make the same mistake that he made several years ago.

What mistake? You discuss these things with him?

Absolutely! We discuss everything and I mean everything except getting him to meet you. The girls are always calling him and willing to "give it up" for him. Danny got sucked in a few years ago and she tried to lay a guilt trip on him. He came to me almost in tears. I straightened him out and especially her. He won't make the same mistake twice. "I'll wait until I genuinely like/love her. We don't even have to be married. Until then, self abuse". He's really a very sensuous, sensible guy. Like his father.

You sure look after Danny.

We look out for each other.

Danny for you? How so?

Shortly after the opening semester of our third year, these vulgar boys started making these rude, vulgar comments along with obscene gestures as Pat and I walked to school .They would follow behind us— too closely. At first we ignored them. Then they became even bolder, threatening. Mom said take Danny with you which we did. "Looky looky, they brought their body guard with them". Danny calmly walked over with a smile and said to the pack leader:" I know that you guys like pretty girls but your comments are upsetting my sister and her friend".

"Well what are you going to do about it, pretty boy"?

Danny doubled him up with a vicious punch to his liver which dropped him to his knees, then to the ground holding his abdomen and writhing in pain. Looking at his cohorts if they were going to help, which they didn't, —they took a few steps backward— he squatted and told him:" if you ever so much as bother my sister and her friend again, I won't be so nice next time". They never bothered us or any of the girls—we never saw them again.

I never knew that Danny was rough.

He's not. He's very gentle, tender. When I first started baby sitting he wanted to come along: "one day I'll be married and I'll want to know how to change a diaper and feed a baby from a bottle. And he was very gentle playing with older kids. You'll feel very protected with Danny.

Cindy, promise me that you'll be my sister even if things don't work out with Danny.

Alice, I promise you that I will and they will work out. Just be open, honest, communicative, affectionate with each other.

Hello sir, I'm here for Alice. We're to go biking this morning.

You're Danny. Come in son. Alice is finishing a few things with her mother and will be down shortly. Would you like a drink, Danny?

Water would be fine, sir.

(Two glasses are brought in)

Thank you.

Alice tells me that you're an honour student and should have no problem being accepted into the course and college of your choice. Have you decided yet?

That's kind of Alice to have said that. I love working with the land and especially with my parents and sister and we both intend to study landscape architecture. You must have heard of Jill's Landscape Architecture?

Yes I have. Your reputation for creative design and integrity is well known in the community.

Thank you. I will pass that on to my parents and Cindy. Oh! I forgot to bring a business card.

(Smiling) That's okay Danny.

My mom is the creative genius. My dad, in addition to being a graduate of honour English had a fairly good business background in construction and is the administrator and project manager. This enabled Jill to be a stay-at-home mom.

Alice should have been down by now. (Calling up gently) Alice, a lady shouldn't keep a gentleman waiting....too long.

I'm coming down now, dad..

(Alice comes down the stairs in her bike shorts which emphasizes her trim muscular legs and figure. Danny eyes glaze momentarily then feels warm in his body)

(Kissing her father) Bye dad. Let's go Danny.

Alice, this patch of trees back from the road is a good place to park the bikes and get us into the shade. Boy it's hot and humid. (wiping their brows after removing their headbands).

Danny, there's a clearing back about 50 feet from the road. The sun's shining through the canopy. Let's wheel our bikes over there and set up our picnic. It looks magical, enchanting.

(Setting up the blanket) Let's get the food (removes the basket from her rat trap). Sitting cross-legged and facing each other and eating slowly. No conversation for a few minutes).

(Danny and Alice get out their guitars and start to tune them). Alice, I love you. I never thought that I would feel that

way about a woman at my age. Thought that you have to be older.

I feel the same way Danny. I feel so comfortable, easy and protected being with you.

Alice, I will always be that way for you.

Danny, if you're ready for the real thing this time so am I.

(Gulps) I am but I've not come prepared. I don't even carry condoms.

I've been prepared as of last month when I started on the pill. That's what I love about you; you're very considerate and thoughtful.

Alice, aside from one misadventure way back that Cindy helped me resolve, there's been no one else. Never wanted anyone else until we met. I love you Alice.

Danny dear, there's been no one else… ever. You're the first and last. I love you Danny.

I've come to ask you both for Alice's hand in marriage. I know this sounds old fashioned but it reflects the respect that I have for you both. Alice and I love each other and what's more, we're great friends.

(Giving an I'm going along with it glance to his wife) Danny, what are your prospects?

(Picking it up and keeping focused). Cindy and I are essentially running the business and we've all agreed to buy mom and dad out in five years—they've accepted our business plan and buy-out proposal. Mom and dad, as you know, have worked likeTrojans building up the business and want to travel. I intend to build a house on our farm, as Cindy and her husband Taggart have already done. Our house will have a music studio so that Alice could continue her teaching and tutoring.

How'd it go?
Fantastic honey? They gave us their blessing. By the way,

do you mind me calling you honey? Dad calls mom hon or honey. She calls him dear or dearest and beast when she thinks that we're out of earshot. It's not that I lack imagination but it's something dear, warm and special to me.

Of course not dearest! By the way, do you want us to be pregnant when we're married? (pinning Danny down by his shoulders on the sofa and running her hair over his face).

Closing his eyes and savouring, then stopping) Holy shit Alice! I told your parents that I respect them and you being pregnant would make me a liar in their eyes.

Oh well, let's keep on practicing. They'll all count nine months when the baby arrives.

CHAPTER 14

NINE MONTHS AND NINE DAYS LATER AT HOME SITTING BESIDE ALICE SLEEPING IN BED

Sleep dearest Alice sleep. It was a hard delivery and both you and Jessica are healthy and home. We've been blessed. Sleep dearest. I have two women in my life to love. Jessica dearest, you're a child of your mother's and father's love for each other and now you've arrived hopefully with the gentle soul that we prayed for every day before and during your mother's pregnancy. Dearest Alice, to see you nourishing Jessica, giving her the sustenance to live is beyond what I can describe. I can't put words to my emotions. Sleep dearest. I'll be here for you both when you awake. I'll love, comfort and protect you both as long as I live.

CHAPTER 15

A FEW DAYS LATER

Hi mom, dad. Your granddaughter Jessica is now receiving.

Hello dear (Jill hugging Alice firmly and sincerely then holding her apart by the arms and looking at her with tears. Jack hugs Danny firmly).

Your mom and dad should be arriving in ten minutes said Jill. We had breakfast together but they had to return as your mom forgot her medication. Cindy and Tagg will be coming over soon withTagg junior.

Oh! That must be their pickup arriving in the driveway.

Hi Cindy (Danny and Cindy hug). Hi Tagg (Danny and Tagg hug firmly. There are tears with both).

Danny, I met the most decent of young man a few weeks ago. His family moved here from the city and he's in my dance class after school.

That's a surprise Alice. I thought that the boys in school were too immature for you and believe me they are.

Not Taggart—everyone calls him Tagg. He's bright, sensitive, a good athlete, intending to study English at college then on to journalism. He reminds me of dad in a way but different in his own way.

When will we meet him, Cindy? (To himself. If he thinks

that he's going to fuck my sister and ditch her, I'll kick the shit out of him).

If he ever gets out of hand or is heading that way Cindy, I'll pay him a visit.

Danny, I know exactly what you're thinking and the words your using and don't you dare and he won't.

Ah yeah, you're probably right, sis (biting his lips gently, smiling and feeling slightly chastised). You're the most intuitive, good judge of character that I've ever met. In fact I'm anxious to meet him.

In time. Remember how mom tested dad with an invite for a "roll in the hay?

Yeah!

It was amazing! I did the same as mom as a test, mind you and he responded almost word for the way dad did. It blew mom away when I told her. "Grab him" was her comment, before someone else does.

I remember how we met, quite by accident.

Oh excuse me. Do you know where the mini-gym is?
I certainly do. I'm going past it. You're new here.
Yes, we moved from the city last week.
Why the mini-gym?

I want to do some tramp work. We were too busy packing for the move and I hadn't worked out for a while and don't want to de-condition too much. By the way, my name is Taggart but everyone calls me Tagg. May I know your name?

You certainly may. My name is Cindy.

Here we are, Tagg.

Thank you Cindy. I'll get changed. Say would you like to meet me for a tea or coffee in about an hour?

I'm meeting a friend then but here's my telephone number Tagg. Call me and we'll get together.

So that's why you didn't prepare dinner that day. "Danny,

I'll be home late. Please cover for me and I'll make it up to you".

Hi Cindy, I don't know whether you remember me. My name is Tagg and you walked me to the mini-gym a few days ago.

Of course I remember you Tagg. How'd your workout go? You said that you were rusty.

Rusty all right! But I started to come around. Cindy, would you like to go for a tea or coffee after school tomorrow?

I'd love to. If it's a good day, would you mind going for a walk? There are so many scenic, walking, hiking trails in the area otherwise tea and coffee are fine.

Why don't we decide tomorrow? I'll meet you at the bike rack.

It's a bright sunny day, Cindy. A walk seems like a healthy activity and I'm okay with it. Are you?

I am Tagg. Let's bike over to a walking trail about 10 minutes by bike. Is your water bottle topped up?

Thanks for asking Cindy. I'll check. Yes it is. Let's go.

(Arriving at the walking trail). Cindy, let's lock our bikes around this tree.

Tagg, what are your plans for this year?

Dad is a lawyer and his firm moved him to town to set up a branch office. He was a small-town boy and wanted badly to leave the city. Mom's his secretary. I have an older sister studying engineering at college. We're here for the long haul Cindy. College? I want to study English lit then go in to journalism.

My dad was a graduate of Honour English but due to circumstances didn't go into the Masters and Ph.D. program. He worked as a fireman until he met mom on a blind date. They fell in love after a 10 day courtship, which was hilarious, then went to work in mom's landscaping business. My brother Danny and I will go into Landscape Architecture.

It's great to share family history Cindy. Cindy! Listen to that beautiful thrush song. (They sit and listen. No conversation for about five minutes).

Cindy, are you okay to move on?

Yes!

Tagg extends his hand to Cindy and helps her up. Cindy stumbles and falls into Tagg who steadies her and is slightly embarrassed.

I'm sorry Cindy if I pulled you up too vigorously.

It's okay Tagg. For a dancer, I lost my balance.

You're a dancer? I took jazz, ballet and acrobatic back in the city and am looking for classes in town.

So that's when you decided he was for you sis?

He certainly had my attention but it really wasn't the dancing. I was getting great vibes from him. When I stumbled and fell against him, he could have become sexually forward but didn't. He was embarrassed. He's very decent and gentle.

Sounds like a very decent guy. I'm starting to like him more and more.

We continued dating, nothing heavy developed   but I sensed that we were becoming very attracted to each other. I decided to take him to our hut where I used mom's strategy and you know what happened. We did become intimate a few days later—we simply couldn't hold off. Why suppress the most beautiful, fundamental human urge. The first time for both of us.

It's a bit hard for me to hear that from my sister, coughed Danny. Hmmm. I smell marriage.

Too soon to tell but I'm hoping.

CHAPTER 16

A FEW MONTHS LATER

Danny dear, we've walked the farm many times but have never been in the hut in the woods at the very back— in the clearing. Why haven't we?

It's mom's and dad's sacred retreat, a place where they would go to be intimate, for quiet, to meditate. It was made available to Cindy and me when appropriate. It's in that hut where they first felt the energy together, where they realized they had strong feelings and cared for each other. They sat on the bench, knees touching innocently with no words passing between them. They both rose and hugged as though it were choreographed. It was before they had their famous manure fight.

(giggling) A manure fight. How romantic!

It's really sensuous.

How so?

Hand me Jessica as it's a bit of a hike. (Taking Jessica and the sling).

Mom wanted to test whether dad was there for a "one-night-stand". She was certain he wasn't but decided to test him anyway as she did others. She walks across the manure in the drive shed with her shit-kicking boots and looks at dad's reflection through the window on the opposite wall. She sees him bending over presumably to lace his hiking boots. He calls her and as she turns around, he heaves a horse-ball at her. She quickly sees the game and flings one back at him. Then they kept at it until they fell into each others arms laughing hysterically. After that, dad took 10 days leave of work to be and work with mom in order to see if they were really in love. And they were.

Wow! Not your typical love story.

That's where dad and I discussed the, don't laugh now, "birds and the bees".

(giggling) How was it? What did you discuss? Sounds exciting!

It was a lot of things: embarrassing initially, fun, learning, sharing.

Embarrasing? How so?

Honey, you're a 13 year old boy and starting to ogle girls and your mother especially notices me ogling Cindy's girl-friends and is washing my crusted bed-sheets (Alice giggling) and underpants— her signal for dad to speak with me.

Tell me more!

We spoke of ethics, responsibility, tenderness. And wacking off.

(From a giggle to a deep laugh). Wacking off?

Yes! Told me to try it with oil to enhance the session.

(Alice had to stop to catch her breath from laughing).Go on. Don't let me stop you.

We talked about liking the girl, not to engage in casual sex and making certain that we both were ready for it; birth control, tenderness, consideration, foreplay which... (interrupted)

Foreplay?

I had never heard of it and had dad explain.

My little Dahny so naïve, so inexperienced?

Yah, I guess so. We spoke about wet dreams and he shared his experiences.

Wet dreams too? This is hysterical!

Yah. Here we are. Let's go in.

Are we allowed?

Yes we are!

Danny, the energy here is strong.

I should have shared this with you years ago.

All three of us are here now. But dear, why the mattress and an upholstered bench? Sir, have you lured me here to mattress or bench me with our child witnessing the deed?

I give choices, miss. Mattress or bench. You choose. By the way, there's a comfy crib in the corner.

Why you devious, horny bugger.

You rang?

I love our life together, Danny. Never did I dream that I would be as happy as we are. A healthy happy daughter, we've become successful in our careers, we're great friends and we sure get along sexually. Cindy is the sister to me that I never had. We're so close that it hurts. Get married, good sex, have kids, grow old together. That's as far as my fantasy would take me as a girl. There never was any other guy for me than you Danny. I still get a smile thinking about our first dance together. When you...

Don't remind me. Came in my pants. I was too much in shock to enjoy the sensation. Your hair across my face still makes my blood boil as though boiled in oil. Aside from an encounter with a girl early on, there was no one else. I promised Cindy that it would be with someone I genuinely cared for. You, dear Alice, were the one. I hear that I was set up. Is that correct?

Yes! Can't tell a lie. It was Cindy's idea.

Now who's the devious one?

You rang?

(Danny whispers). Alice, Jess is sleeping.

(Whispers back) You don't have to whisper. Give me a minute you animal.

CHAPTER 17

FIVE YEARS LATER.
CHRISTMAS EVE AT ALICE'S
AND DANNY'S

(Jack and Jill arrive. Jill shakes the snow from her coat and Danny takes it. Jill sits on a stool and removes her boots with a grunt).

Brrrr it's freezing. According to the weather reports, there's lots of cold, ice and sleet which will make driving treacherous tonight said Jill.

(Jack has an armful of gifts which he hands to Danny who places them under the tree. Jack removes his boots, his coat which he shakes and hands it to Danny who is waiting for it. They all hug warmly). Randy, Audrey and the kid's are spending Christmas with her folks in Arizona, said Jack. Her father is not well and might not be around for next Christmas. They all send their love and will join us next year. I saw Gord and Belinda's car in the driveway. Where are they hiding?

They're in the studio with Jess who's showing them her new dance routine, replied Danny. She couldn't wait to show them. "I'll do it again for grandpa, grandma Jack and

Jill when they arrive and for aunt and uncle Cindy, Tagg and junior when they get here".

Good thing that Gord and Belinda arrived early, said Jack. Their room is ready and they are not driving back tonight. We'll have a family brunch around 10:00AM and they can be on their way anytime thereafter, weather permitting.

Wait! I hear Cindy and Tagg's truck pulling up, said Jack.

Excuse me mom, dad but I've got to get back to the kitchen to help Alice. Won't be long. Join us in the kitchen.

Son, it's redolent of exquisite cookery, remarked Jack.

The cake looks scrumptious. What is it, dear? asked Jill.

You'll love it! It's a sugar and gluten free garbanzo bean chocolate cake. Get your fingers off it Danny. (Slapping them gently).

(Gord and Belinda come in with Jess. Jess runs and jumps up to Jack and they hug, then to Jill. They all hug.

Jill, Jack. You should have seen Jess do her routine. Now it's your return. Actually we want to see it again. Jess, is it okay?

Of course grandpa Gord.

(Cindy, Tagg and Tagg junior walk in and start removing their winter gear. Jess runs over and hugs them all individually). Come into the studio, I have a new dance routine that I'm going to do as soon as you all change. Junior, how's your tap lessons going?

Well, not so good, Jess. I guess I got two left feet. Maybe I'll try acrobatic dancing that mom and dad used to do.

(The show is over. There is enthusiastic applause. Everyone hugs Jess).

That was terrific, said junior. I'll consider acrobatics in the new year.

Hey dear hearts! said Danny. We'll serve dinner buffet

style; the plates, silverware, food are in the kitchen and we'll eat in the dining room.

(When everyone is seated). Gord, this year it's your turn to say grace, said Danny.

Thank you Danny. (All bow their heads). How wonderful and blessed are we to be able to gather with all our loved ones, to share in the food prepared with love. In your name.

(After dinner and clean up)

Let's all retire to then family room for carol singing, conversation, music and simply to enjoy each others company, said Danny.

Alice, are you sure that it's wise to go to the community centre in the morning? said Jill aside. It's treacherous. The roads are icy and the visibility isn't too good.

Thanks Jill for your concern, Jill. If the weather and roads are still treacherous, we won't go but I'm sure that the road crews will have the roads cleared and salted. There'll be a pancake breakfast for Jess's class and she is to receive an award for her dance routine. We have to get there by eight and will be back around 10:00 AM to join you all for brunch.

That's okay dear, said Belinda. Just drive carefully, have your cell-phone fully charged.

Thank you mother. I also have a winter pack in the van which will enable us to keep warm, fed and safe for a few days.

Thanks dear. A parent always worries about her children regardless of their ages.

(Alice on piano and voice leads all in carol singing).

Hey Jack, interrupted Gord, how's that Rocky Top number that you and Danny were working on?

If you want a break from the carol singing: we've got some work to do on it but it's presentable. Danny, are you up to it?

Sure thing, dad. I'll get your guitar and my banjo.

(They tune their instruments with Alice on piano giving them a "d".

Jack nods to Danny and they begin
Wish that I was on ole rocky top,
Down in the tennessee hills.
Aint no smoggy smoke on rocky top,
Aint no telephone bills.
Once there was a girl on rocky top,
Half bear the other half cat.
Wild as a mink, sweet as soda pop,
I still dream about that.
Rocky top, youll always be
Home sweet home to me.
Good ole rocky top,
Rocky top tennessee, rocky top tennessee.
Once two strangers climbed on rocky top,
Lookin for a moonshine still.
Strangers aint come back from rocky top,
Guess they never will.
Corn wont grow at all on rocky top
Dirts too rocky by far.
Thats why all the folks on rocky top
Get their corn from a jar.
Rocky top, youll always be
Home sweet home to me.
Good ole rocky top,
Rocky top tennessee, rocky top tennessee.
Now Ive had years of cramped up city life,
Trapped like a duck in a pen.
Now all I know is its a pity life
Cant be simple again.
Rocky top, youll always be
Home sweet home to me.
Good ole rocky top,
Rocky top tennessee, rocky top tennessee.

Rocky top tennessee, rocky top tennessee.
Yeah rocky top tennesee eee eee eee.

(Everyone applauds vigorously)

Alice, said Jill lovingly, it's getting late and before we get ready for bed, please sing us a song. You have a beautiful rich voice.

I'd love to, said Alice. (Sits at the piano, thinks for a moment). Danny, please sit on the bench with me. I've never sung this before and now is the time, my love.

Oh Danny boy, the pipes, the pipes are calling
From glen to glen, and down the mountain side
The summer's gone, and all the flowers are dying
'Tis you, 'tis you must go and I must bide.
But come ye back when summer's in the meadow
Or when the valley's hushed and white with snow
'Tis I'll be here in sunshine or in shadow
Oh Danny boy, oh Danny boy, I love you so.
And if you come, when all the flowers are dying
And I am dead, as dead I well may be
You'll come and find the place where I am lying
And kneel and say an "Ave" there for me.
And I shall hear, tho' soft you tread above me
And all my dreams will warm and sweeter be
If you'll not fail to tell me that you love me
I'll simply sleep in peace until you come to me.
I'll simply sleep in peace until you come to me.

(There was silence then a warm applause. Danny kisses Alice as does Jess).

Brunch at 10:00 AM, said a tired Danny.

CHAPTER 18

Don't wake daddy, Jess. Let's get dressed, whispered Jill.

Mommy, I'm so excited about getting an award. And when we come back, I'll show it to everyone.

I'm so happy for you dear. Start getting dressed while I warm up the van and scrape off the ice. Be back in 10-15 minutes.

(Brunch at 10:00AM the following morning)

Jack dear, said Jill. Alice should have been back by now.

You're right. Let me call her on her cell. (Dials). No answer. There are some "no cell-phone service areas on her way home.

(There's a knock on the door and Danny answers it)

Yes officers, come in. Can we get you some breakfast? Coffee?

Thank you but we've had our breakfast. Are you the owner of the 2006 Dodge Ram?

Why yes, said a nervous, apprehensive Danny,

It's our unpleasant duty to inform you.....

CHAPTER 19

AFTER APRIL AND JESS'S DEATH AND FUNERAL. DANNY IN THE HUT

(Crying) I can't face life without Alice and Jess. I've never felt hurt, emptiness, loneliness, depression as this. (loads the revolver points it to his temple and as he is about to squeeze the trigger...

"No! daddy, No! Don't do it!

What the? Who?

We don't have too much time. Listen to your daughter, Danny. (A vision of Alice and Jessica appear before Danny)

Danny dearest, I know that you're hurt in the worst way possible in human form. Killing yourself will not assure you of joining us.

That's true daddy.

You will get over the hurt in the years to come and will marry a woman who will be good for you and you for her. You'll both have a good life together. She will have a daughter whom you will learn to love as your own and adopt. Jess and I will always reside in your heart and soul until you pass on and join us. It will never interfere in your relationship with that woman and her daughter. Commune with us as often as you need just as your mom and dad have done with their mothers. We will not be able to respond directly but might in a manner unknown to you. We have to go now as we were given this brief time with you before we pass on. Goodbye dearest, my love.

Bye daddy, I'll always love you.

(Danny just sat there with his head on the bench for hours weeping)

Danny, may I come? in asked Tagg.

What? Waking up. Sure Tagg, come in.

Feel like talking Danny? If you don't that's cool. (notices the revolver but doesn't mention it).

Danny, (composing himself) I was going to blow my brains out. I hurt so badly, feel so empty emotionally and rock bottom depressed. I feel as though my heart was gouged from me. I couldn't go on. As I was about to pull the trigger and blow my brains out, Alice and Jess came to me in a vision—I actually saw them as I last remember them. Alice had on her favourite skirt and blouse and Jess had those earrings I had bought for her before the accident. Jess said "daddy no"! Then Alice spoke to me, can't recall the words, probably locked in my memory somewhere. They gave me the strength to continue.

And I will. Tagg, your like a dear brother and I love you for being so supportive. If it weren't for you and Cindy, I would have blown my brains out a few days ago.

Tagg, (jokingly) we need you in the business to help pay off your mom and dad. Then blow them out.

Danny smiled for the first time since the funeral. Let's go but first, bro, a hug.

CHAPTER 20

FOUR YEARS LATER

Isn't it time that you started dating again? asked Cindy as she and Danny were cleaning the dishes after dinner.

Cindy, I'm afraid that I wouldn't know what to say, what to do with another woman.

Danny dear, you're projecting, fantasizing negatively and it's normal.

Alice was your one and only love and the thought of making love to another women must be either frightening or adulterous in your mind.

All the above, sis. I'm scared, terrified.

Do you think Alice, if she were looking in on you, would not want to see you happy with another woman?

I guess you're right sis.

You might be interested in this article, said Tagg, that I read on-line from the city newspaper. Attention Egyptologists. Egypt comes to the city at the museum. That's one of your hobbies. Why not go there?

You can never tell what might happen, said Cindy. Serendipity?

I have to be in the city for a few days to check out the Mill Stream Project and the condos by the river. I'll visit the museum. I have so many questions to ask the curator.

That's what we want to hear said Cindy and Tagg.

Janice, you're baby-sitter is sick and I have an important meeting at the museum. Take your homework with you. I'm certain that there's a quiet room near our room where you could do your homework.

Do I haaave to go, mommy?

Yes you do. If I leave you alone the Children's Aid will come after me.

But you're a responsible operating room nurse. Why would they bother you?

If they feel that you've been neglected, that I'm a bad mother, I'll have to take time off work and hire a lawyer which we can't afford. When your father died without life insurance—I assumed that he had auto insurance because I left finances with him— and lots of debt, it took years for me to pay them off and it's been only recently that I've been able to start saving. It's time and you're old enough to know this. This is not for debate so please get in the car and we'll have dinner at your favourite restaurant.

Goody! What are we waiting for?

Thank you professor for clarifying some odd notions that I had about Hatshepsut. Some woman! The display was absolutely stunning, informative, educational. And thank you for your e-mail address. I'll certainly be in touch. Now if you'll excuse me professor, I have to fight the city gridlock to get home—I've got a three hour drive through deer country.

Looking forward to hearing from you Danny.

You will professor!

(Walking out to the rotunda) Danny, what brings you here? asked Mabel his neighbour down the road. She was divorced, they were good friends and knew that it would never go beyond that).

(They hug) Tagg told me of the Egyptology display and

I made some interesting notes and discoveries. I'm so glad he told me about it.

Look Danny, I have to get home right away. My baby sitter called—George has a fever. There is a singles group upstairs and you might find someone. Here's my ticket.

Mabel, I've haven't shaved for the two days that I've been in the city, I'm wearing my old woodsman's shirt with old jeans. I'm hardly a candidate for meeting a woman. What's going on?

I believe a debate between a minister and a psychologist on religion and reality. Go. Trust in serendipity.

Ohhkay, Mabel, (breathing out deeply). I'll give it a shot even though I look like I've rolled out of a boxcar.

(Approaching the door to the singles group) Here's my ticket.

Are you certain that you're in the right meeting? asked the ticket taker arrogantly. The ditch diggers' association is having their AGM on the second floor.

(Smiling to himself). Nope! This is the place. (Walks in and the two women at the door look at each other and shake their heads)

(Asking at a table with men and women). Is this seat available?

A man and woman simultaneously). No! It's reserved for a friend.

(Danny smiles to himself as it repeats itself for several tables. I don't blame them the way I'm dressed. I'll go out this side door and organize my notes somewhere. There's a table where I can spread and collate the handouts and organize my notes. Oh! There's a kid. Looks like she's doing homework. I'll sit far away from her)

(After about 10 minutes the girl speaks) Mr. Are you good in math?

Yes I am, Why do you ask?

I'm so bad in math and I have a test tomorrow and I don't understand the topic.

I'm a stranger. You shouldn't be speaking to me. Your mother, whom I assume is in the meeting, will not approve.

Please mister. I feel that you are a nice man.

Why thank you sweety. (Oops, I shouldn't have said sweety said Danny to himself) Let's review the topic together.

(After about 30' minutes.) There you go. You answered the five questions assigned perfectly. You now know your stuff. I guess that you never knew that you were good in math.

(Shakes her head with a smile)

What are you doing with my daughter? Get out of here before I call security.

But mother!

But nothing!

I was merely…

Get out before I call 911 and security.

Very well, I'll gather my papers and leave.

Good!

CHAPTER 21

Tagg, thanks for suggesting the museum. The collection was spectacular, the curator extremely informative—we'll communicate by internet.

Mabel told me that she gave you her ticket to a singles meeting. How'd it go?

It didn't. I almost got thrown in jail. I looked like I rolled out of a box car and when I asked to sit at table after table, they rejected me like I had cholera. Couldn't blame them the way I looked so I went outside to organize my notes. When I had finished and about to leave, this sweet little girl who was at the other end of the table pleaded with me to help her with math. She would have been Jess's age, had her colouring and build which freaked me. I did help her. Then when her mother came out to get her, all hell broke loose. She threatened to call security, 911 if I didn't leave immediately. Neither I nor the girl could explain. I don't blame the mother. What with child molesters and perverts in the news, she was being protective of her daughter.

Anyway, how'd it go at the mall?

We finished phase three two days ahead and the project manager is pleased.

Wonderful! Danny, to change the subject. My buddy Mack is a TV host who interviews interesting people. For his next show he will be interviewing men/women whose spouses along with child or children were killed in auto accidents and how they got their lives back on track. I asked him to call you as a possible interviewee.

Whew!! (Breathing out heavily). I don't know Tagg how I'll feel reliving it although I feel that it's well-behind me. Okay! I think I can handle it.

Danny, Tagg and I are so proud of the way you came out of it. From wanting to blow your brains out to an almost—I say almost because you haven't been with a woman— perfectly functioning, decent, giving man.

CHAPTER 22

Janice. Please turn on channel 500 in five minutes. I'll join you then.

What's on, mommy?

It's a program on how people put their lives together after their spouse and a child or children were killed in an auto accident. It started about 10 minutes ago.

Mommy. Daddy was killed in an auto accident. He wasn't the best daddy but he was my daddy and I still miss him. I don't want to cry.

You don't have to watch it. Please put it on and call me so that I could watch it.

Okay mommy.

It's on mommy.

Before the commercial you heard the inspiring stories of William and Catherine who were able to put their lives together. Grief counseling, inter-personal counseling, family, friends and community support all played an important part in their rehab. Jo-Anne. You have a unique story.

Yes I do Mack. I had Mary when I was in my early thirties. Sid and I were thrilled at the prospect of having a daughter. The birth was okay and Mary was healthy. Then it all vanished in a flash by a drunken driver.

Jo-Anne let me interject briefly. All stories that we've

heard tonight involve drunken drivers. Sorry Joanne. Please continue.

Thank you Mack. I isolated myself for months. Didn't want any counseling of any sort. My friends dropped off food and tried to console me. Not by offering advice or making small talk. Just being there, present with me. If we spoke, I forget about what. Fairly soon I asked for and received counseling which helped enormously. I went back to work after counseling. Then one Friday I took off early from work and went shopping at the supermarket and then it hit me like a sledge hammer on my temple. In the line to pay and behind a mother with her daughter, laughing, talking, joking, adjusting her daughter's braid. I ran to my car leaving my cart full of groceries where I went into hysterics with no husband or anyone to console or comfort me. I was able to drive home where I sat in the dark for hours. After that I went shopping at night in 24 hour supermarkets which I did until three years ago when I found a wonderful supportive man. We were married and I became pregnant immediately and gave birth to a beautiful girl whom I take shopping with me as we can afford for me to be a stay at home mom which is the greatest gift parents can give their children if they are so inclined or financially able which is challenging for most. We're hardly rich but we re-arranged our lives, finances to accomplish it.

(Mack with genuine tears) Jo-Anne that was so inspiring how you were able to overcome your grief. Your husband and daughter are in the audience. Mort and Abby, stand up. (They stand and the audience applauds).

Thank you Joanne. Danny. (The camera focuses on Danny) You lost wife and five year old daughter about four years ago.

There's the nice man Mommy who helped me with my math.

(Miriam rushes in from the kitchen wearing her apron, sits down and watches).

(Danny nods. Composes himself) Alice was the love of my life and our daughter Jess (voice wavers but then he controls it) was a child of our love then bang and it's over.

Danny, how did you handle your grief and get your life back in order?

Mack, Alice and my twin sister Cindy had adopted themselves as sisters as teenagers. Cindy took Alice's and Jess's death as hard as I did. Cindy slept with me—nothing sexual—for weeks where we cried and poured our hearts out to each other. Cindy's husband Tagg, who's like a brother to me and my best friend was a rock. I was going to blow my brains out and as I was about to pull the trigger—now this might not be in yours and your viewer's beliefs—Alice and my daughter came back to me in a vision. "Daddy No! said Jess. Then Alice spoke to me and for the life of me, can't recall what she said. But I felt better after that vision. Then Tagg came in and we talked. That was rock bottom and the turn around. Believe me the next few years were the most painful but positive period for me. Grief counselling, family, friends helped enormously. You can tell yourself that it happens every day which is unfortunately true. But when you hear it from fellow human beings at a therapy group, it resonates. Time can heal; it heals better with family and effective therapy. Unlike Jo-Anne, I had a need to get involved with kids especially those around Jess's age. I tutor those who need help with their school work; I'm part of a teacher, parent coach team coaching coed hockey, gym and baseball. We've won some athletic awards and our math team in its first year ranked third in the area.

Coaching, tutoring—surrogate parenting you might say—has been my love. Being in a family business, I was able to make time for the kids only because my sister and brother-in-law covered for me.

Cindy, Tagg, please stand. (Audience applauds vigorously)

Thanks Cindy, Tagg.

Danny, parents of kids that you coach must be grateful.

They are but I had a misunderstanding in the city a while ago. My fault, couldn't help myself and should have known better. This sweet girl—she'd be Jess's age with the same colouring and build which really freaked me out—asked me to help her with math. We happened to share the same table at the museum. I looked like a derelict because I was working around the clock in the city for a few days in order to finish a project so that I could attend the Egyptology display at the museum.

On my dear God! cried Miriam.

Mommy, why are you crying. Now I'm crying too.

(composing herself) Janice dear, there's something about that man. I can't determine what it is. It's affecting me somehow. Sorry. Let's watch.

Then when her mother saw me with her daughter all hell broke loose and I was fortunate not to have to explain matters to a security guard.

Danny, was the woman irrational, angry?

Not at all, Mack. She was a good mother protecting her daughter from a stranger, possibly a pedophile.

Thank you Danny and all you folks who shared your personal inspirational stories.

Janice. I'm going contact Danny via the TV station and apologize to him. Maybe we could invite him to dinner.

CHAPTER 23

Hi Danny, you won't remember me. I'm the irrational angry mother who threatened to call security at the museum.

Of course I remember you. You weren't irrational ma'am. You were protective of your daughter.

Please call me Miriam. Ma'am makes me feel like an old scold.

Miriam, how's your daughter?

Janice is fine and asked me to tell you that she aced the math test but she's slipping back a bit.

Well she's a bright young girl and with the right tutor, will start to be more proficient.

Danny, Janice and I want to invite you for dinner when you're next in the city.

Thank you Miriam. You don't really have to go to that extent. Your telephone call is all that I need.

Danny, we genuinely want to. What's best for you, weekday or weekend?

The weekend would be better for me Miriam.

Us too.

Danny, do you have any food allergies, preferences?

Thanks for asking Miriam. No I don't. I have what you might call a catholic appetite.

Can you make it for say 5:00PM? This way Janice, who wants to thank you, could be up for a while before going to bed and you could return home at a decent hour.

Sounds great. Miriam, please e-mail directions to your home. My address is danny@jackandjill.com. And looking forward to meeting you and Janice....and under better circumstances.

Yes, Danny. With my claws retracted this time. (Both laugh)

CHAPTER 24

Miriam I presume?

Miriam nods

Danny I assume?

Danny nods. It's both of us Miriam.

Please come in.

(Taking off his shoes) You can leave them on, Danny.

Habit Miriam. I prefer it. You and Janice probably spent a lot of energy cleaning your home and it's not my intention to disrespect it.

(Gives Danny a tour of the house) You made a comfortable home for you and Janice, Miriam. I feel good vibes.

(Janice enters. Danny has to restrain himself from hugging her).

Hi Janice. I know that you are a polite girl and not certain how to address me so please call me Danny. If that's okay with you Miriam?

Yes it is. Have a seat Danny.

Janice and I watched the interview and we felt the pain of all the interviewees. My husband died a few years ago. Killed while driving drunk. I was a stay-at- home-mom and he left us highly in debt and with no insurance. Before marriage I was an operating room nurse so when Geoff died I went back to school to upgrade my skills. Not being home for Janice after school saddened me, sickened me, felt guilty— initially.

But, I realized that I was now no different than the millions of single sole support working mothers.

Janice, it must have been hard for you with your mommy not being home when you came from school. How did you feel about it?

Oh Danny, I cried at first wanting my mommy even my daddy to be there. Then I soon realized that's how it had to be from now on. Mommy taught me how to get dinner things ready and we try to keep our home neat and tidy.

I can see. For two working girls, you've done a fantastic job and you should be proud of yourself Janice. How's the math going?

I aced it after you taught me but I'm still having problems with some of the topics.

Excuse me for a minute, Janice I need to talk to your mom.

(Away from Janice). Miriam, would you let me help Janice after dinner? You can sit in on the session.

That's okay Danny. Ordinarily I would ask you to help me with the dishes—I feel comfortable telling you this—but since you'll need the time for Janice and the three hour drive home, I'll agree.

Miriam, I have a suggestion. I drove my camper van here. If it's okay with you, how about the three of us cleaning up after dinner, I'll work with Janice, then sleep in my van. In the AM may I take you and Janice out for breakfast?

We'd love it. We have a guest room that you could sleep in.

It's kind of you to offer but I'll feel more comfortable in my van if I could park it in your driveway. I hope that you understand.

I understand Danny. And the driveway is fine. What time do you want us up?

You tell me.

How's 9:00AM?

Sounds good.

Wow! That was the best home cooked meal that I've had in years, girls. Miriam, if the three of us clean up means that Janice and I could get together sooner for her math.

Sounds good to me!

You've done well Janice and you really know your stuff. It's getting late and I've got to get to bed early as I've had a busy week. Tomorrow you're having breakfast with me, You and your mommy are to choose the restaurant. Good night Janice.

Can I give you a goodnight kiss Danny.

(Restraining himself) Sure thing sweety. (kisses Danny on the cheek and goes to her bedroom.

Goodnight Miriam. See you in the AM. They hug.

(Danny lying in his bed in the van. With tears) Alice dear. Forgive me for hugging Miriam. It felt so good hugging a woman. The hug wasn't supposed to be erotic. It was intended as a non-verbal statement that I enjoyed the evening. Her soft scented hair brushing my face made me feel warm inside. Reminiscent of yours which set me off. There's something about her that I can't really put together. Maybe it will come to me in time. And Jess, it felt so good to have a girl give me a daughter kiss on the cheek. I miss my baby telling me "I love you daddy". I miss you baby. Goodnight my loved ones.

CHAPTER 25

(Rapping on van door) Hey Danny are you ready to roll?

(Through the door). I'm ready Miriam. (Opening the door).Just finished my meditation. Shall we go in your car as the van is messy and you know where you intend to take us? Good morning Janice, did you sleep well?

Much better Danny because I know that my math home work's done and you made it easy for me.

It makes me happy to hear that Janice.

My friends call me Jan, Danny.

Sure thing Jan.

Danny, Jan's favourite breakfast eatery has a New York flavour serving not only your typical breakfast menu but blintzes, lox, cream cheese, pickled, marinated and matjes herring, cheese cakes and the like.

I love the stuff. Miriam, Jan, do the waiters insult you?

Insult? Why no! Why do you ask? inquired Miriam

(Laughing) There's a restaurant in our area famous for that. They insult, mock, put you down, humiliate you. If you don't have a good sense of humour or sense of self or you're too serious, it's not for you.

Oh Mommy, can we visit Danny and go to that restaurant? Sounds like a lot of fun.

Jan, you shouldn't be so forward with Danny. You hardly know him.

Miriam, I feel flattered that Jan trusts me enough to ask

me. If you and Jan like, please consider being my guests one weekend. Discuss it. You don't have to make your decision now. In fact don't make it now. Think about it and I'll call you later this week.

Danny, what about next weekend? asked an excited Jan.

Jan, discuss it with your momma and I'll call you later this week.

(What have I done? said Danny to himself)

Table for three please.

This way. (They all sit)

I know what I want, said Jan without reading the menu.

You certainly know how to make up your made quickly Jan. I'm a bit slower and not familiar with the menu. What are you ordering?

I'm ordering the blueberry blintzes with blueberry jam and a sour cream side. Will that be too expensive Danny?

Absolutely yes! When I can't pay the bill we'll all have to wash, dry the dishes and sweep, vacuum the floor. Like last night.

That's funny, Danny. (Miriam conceals a smile)

Sounds positively delicious, Jan. A bit rich for me though but I'll order the apple blintzes with sour cream—I'm a sour cream freak.

You too Danny? I can eat a container all at once if mommy would let me.

Your mommy knows what's best for you, Jan. How did you feel after you had eaten all that cream?

My tummy felt bad.

Listen to your mommy. She knows what's good for you.

Have you decided Miriam?

Not yet. I like to avoid overly rich foods.

Miriam, that will be a challenge here.

Tell me about it. Hmmm. I think that I'll order the mixed fruit plate and a cup of green tea.

I'll take your orders if you're ready.

(Jan jumps in) I'll have the blueberry blintz…..

That was certainly a deliciously rich meal. I'll have to work it off and go on fluids for a day said a sated Danny.

I'll work harder at my acrobatic dance class, said Jan.

Your what? Sorry Jan, that surprised me. Keeping physically active is very important at all ages. Being young and fit, you won't gain any weight. Miriam, do you dance too?

I take tap whenever I can get away.

I collect musicals which are heavy into dance: modern, ballet and especially tap; oldies: Fred Astaire, Nicholas Brothers, Eleanor Powell, Ann Miller, Gene Kelly, Donald O'Connor and more.

I enjoyed spending this time with both of you. Give thought to visiting me—I'm not pressuring you. It's a three hour drive mostly through deer warning sign country. We have a hundred acres where the air is clean and the water is from a well several hundred feet down. You'll have your own bedroom. (gives them both a hug).

CHAPTER 26

How'd it go, Danny? asked Cindy at the dinner table with Tagg anticipating.

She's a decent, warm, responsible woman and a very caring mother— an operating room nurse. Her daughter Janice—Jan—and I hit it off not that I was expecting to. Actually she hit it off with me. She's Jess's age and has her body and colouring which freaked me out at first. I like her. When she kissed me on my cheek, it reminded me of Jess which nearly tore me apart. Then I settled down. Oh! Her name is Miriam. Her husband must have been an alcoholic—he was killed diving drunk in an auto accident a few years back.

Danny, are you able are you ready to handle a relationship with another woman?—a quality woman if I've heard you correctly.

Don't know, Cindy, I intend to approach it slowly. Jan will be a challenge as she is gung ho to see Miriam and me married. I only spent part of a weekend with them. I'm not infatuated or anything close. I liked what I saw though. There's something about her that I can't figure out. I feel a closeness without really knowing her.

Tell me again: what makes you think that you are ready for a relationship with Miriam?

Hmmm. Cindy, As I said, I don't know whether I am. I find that I'm attracted to her. When I hugged her after saying goodnight and her soft-scented hair brushed my face, I felt things stirring very strongly in me. It's a lot different than Alice where it was like thunder. But then I was ten years younger.

That's a good sign. But Danny, you haven't dated a woman since Alice died. Miriam is the first woman that you've been attracted to. Hugged. How do you know that it's not an infatuation? You go to bed with her for a while, you're like a father to Jan, then one of you decides that it's not working. Perhaps frightened by intimacy. Jan would be devastated. Perhaps angry with Miriam or blame herself. Shouldn't you start dating other woman? Play the field? Bed a few women?—I know lots of women in the area who are just waiting for the call. They ask me every other day when I'm in town.

Sis. For some reason, I don't want to play the field. Miriam is attractive, decent—you know, I've described her to you. I particularly like her daughter Jan. But no, I'm not confusing her with Jess. Yes! I've seen women that I'm attracted to but that's where it ends. I've even had coffee, dinner dates with a few in the past month. Nothing! Didn't tell you about it because they were non-events. At first I felt that I was betraying Alice but realized that it was foolish even though I still commune with her and Jess. It's really too early but I want to give it an honest effort.

I feel better with your response and respect it. If you both decide to become intimate and you're afraid that you won't be able to get it up and all that, tell her your feelings, your fears. She probably has her own fears, issues which she may or not share with you. "Can we just hug each other"? you might say. Don't put pressure on yourself—or on Miriam as well. Try penetration when you're confident and only then and you are certain that she's ready. If she's the woman that I feel she is, she'll understand, even respect you for your honesty.

Sis, you're lifted a mill-stone from my shoulders as the thought of having sex with another woman has me scared shitless. Getting it up after these years….shit, I never had trouble before, why should I with Miriam if it even goes that far? I'm fantasizing, projecting. I'm stopping it now.

Great! But, go slow as I suggested. Danny, most women can fight another woman for a man but they can't or won't fight a ghost.

I hear you sis. I'm also very relieved that you brought it up.

That's what I'm here for.

That's what you're here for? When I told them about Crudite' Jan jumped on it and wanted to go to be insulted. Funny. I then asked them to consider coming up for a weekend.

We're anxious to meet Miriam and Jan, said Tagg. By the way. We decided that we want to have a child and Cindy is three months pregnant.

Fantastic! You finally knocked up my sister. I was getting worried about you. I'm thrilled! I'm overjoyed! Delirious! I'll be an uncle! Do mom and dad know?

We're telling them when they return from France this week.

That's right! In two days. That should cure their jet-lag.

CHAPTER 27

Hi Miriam. Danny here. I had an enjoyable time with you and Jan.

And we enjoyed having you stay with us.

Have you decided about visiting me?

Jan has her bag packed.

What about Miriam?

Danny, I'm afraid.

(Pauses for a few seconds). Miriam, I have my fears as well. You're the first woman I've hugged after Alice died. It wasn't meant to be erotic. Just a non-verbal statement that I enjoyed the evening. And you know something? It was beautiful: feeling, smelling, sensing another woman's energy, embracing her. Alice and I were so close it hurt. I doted on my daughter Jess. Then gone in a flash. I've been mourning her all these years but aware that my realty is that they're gone. You haven't had it easy either. Settling Geoff's debts, going back to school, worrying about Jan—not being at home for her when she's back from school. You've had your own hell to deal with as well. Now yours and Jan's lives are stable and predictable. Miriam, there will be nothing heavy if you can trust me. My twin sister Cindy and husband Tagg are looking forward to meeting you and Jan. Cindy and Alice adopted each other as sisters in high school and was just as devastated as I was at losing my family. (Miriam hears the emotion in Danny's voice).

Danny, Jan and I will drive up Saturday. We'll leave at 8:00AM and should arrive circa 11:00 A.M. ish provided I don't hit a deer.

We're all looking forward to it Miriam. Drive carefully.

(Danny to himself. What have I done? What am I doing? What am I possibly opening up here? I've reconciled myself to the reality that there never will be another Alice and Jess in my life. But there's something about Miriam that I can't figure out. My body feels good about her but I can't wrap my mind around it. Jan is a delight. She's the closest to Jess as I can imagine.)

(Miriam to herself. What am I doing? Do I need a man in my life now? Ever? My life is stable. I enjoy my job. It's secure, my employers like and respect me. Debts paid off, starting to save. Jan is settled in a good school and is a happy child. What happens if he's irresponsible like Geoff. A drunk as well. He seems to be a healthy, responsible, involved man. I was touched by his openness on TV. What happens if he's not attracted to me or rejects Jan. Actually when he hugged me, I felt loving energy. And he and Jan really hit it off. Especially Jan who dearly would love to have a decent father in her life. A responsible male role model. Loosen up girl. He's a good man. There's something about him that I can't get my mind around. It's a positive feeling though. Oh well!)

CHAPTER 28

Miriam, Jan, welcome to our homestead. I'm Cindy, Danny's sister.

(The two women observe, size each other up. Now women have the uncanny ability to sniff each other out in a flash to determine how, whether and to what extent they will relate to each other.)

They hug each other firmly. And you are Jan. May I hug you, Jan?

Jan nods shyly and they hug.

Come into our house and meet my husband Tagg. Danny will be over in about five minutes—he's parking the "dozer".

Tagg, let me introduce you to Miriam and her beautiful daughter Jan.

(Jan blushes)

Great to meet you. May I give you both a collective hug?

(Miriam looks at Jan who nods shyly. Tagg gives them a warm hug).

You've had a long drive. Would you like some tea and home-made short bread cookies just out of the oven? Lunch will be in about an hour or so.

I'd love some tea and home made short breads. I don't have much time for baking now that I'm working full-time.

Oh mommy. Short bread cookies are my favourite!

Then you shall have them. But listen to mommy as to how many you should eat. We don't want you eating so many that your tummy will feel like it's bursting at the seams.

(Danny comes in) Hi Miriam hi Jan. Jan runs to give him a hug.

(Danny and Jan hug).

Hi Miriam. (They shake hands not knowing how else to great each other, their eyes looking away slightly). How was the drive up?

It was an extremely scenic drive with granite rock, an impressive mix of greenery and beautiful lakes.

I saw some deer on the side of the road and a bear running across the highway said an excited Jan.

There's lots of wild animals in the area, dear, said Cindy. If you want to see bears feasting, we'll go to the dump. Excuse me for a moment. I'll serve the tea and cookies.

Oh mommy, can we go?

Aren't they wild and dangerous, Danny?

They can be Miriam. But if you stand well back there's no real danger as the bears just want to eat. The dump manager is a sharp-shooter and he'll know whether there's a threat. Has a rifle in his shed. If you like, we could go later in the afternoon before the dump closes or tomorrow, perhaps.

Here are the tea and the short breads. (Cindy brings then in on a silver platter along with bone china teacups. Pours tea for everyone). Help yourselves.

Jan, please take one for now, said Miriam.

We don't want you getting a tummy ache by eating too many, said Danny.

Those were the most welcome, delicious cookies and tea especially after the ride up, said Miriam.

They were yummy, Cindy.

Why thank you. Let me show you to your room in our house. Danny's house is a stone's throw down the road.

You'll have a comfortable king-sized bed for you with a warm duvet. If it gets cold for you at night, the thermostat for the propane fireplace is on the wall next to the door. Your towels are on the dresser and the bathroom is down the hall on the right. There's a sauna and a jacuzzi tub for you as well.

We don't have a lock on the door. When you're in the bathroom, simply hang the occupied sign out on the door knob. I'll leave you for a few minutes as I'm sure that you want to rest, freshen up and change.

Thank you Cindy.

Jan flops on the bed which seems to swallow her. Mommy, it's so comfortable. We haven't slept together for a long time.

Too long dear. Let's enjoy it tonight—woman to woman.

Let's rest for about 15 minutes, get changed and join them.

Mommy, they all like to hug and must love each other very much. Daddy never hugged me much and neither did grandma and grandpa. I feel so good when they do.

So do I dear. I like the family and especially Cindy.

Danny, Miriam's a lovely woman and Jan is a sweety. Go slo bro!

I intend to sis. I have to.

I want to talk to her, get to know her better, said Cindy. I seem to be getting strange but positive vibes myself. Just started. Interesting!

It was a great idea putting Miriam and Jan in your house. I feel that she is relieved as well. Oh! Here they come.

You girls look refreshed said Danny happily.

Thanks Danny, I needed to rest and freshen up after that scenic drive up.

Danny, will you help me with my homework this

weekend. There's my math of course and a poem that I don't understand. Maybe we could read it together.

(Glancing to Miriam who nodded). I'd love to Jan.

Miriam. Why don't you and I clean up after dinner so that Danny and Jan could work together, suggested Cindy.

And I've got to work on some accounts. (Tagg noted Cindy's expression which said clear out).

That was a delicious dinner, Cindy. It's some comfort not having to prepare dinner. (Washing, cleaning, wiping together).

Miriam. I love my brother Danny dearly. We've been as close as a brother and sister can be. His wife Alice was a dear, dear—starts to sob then stops—sister. We were devastated when she died. That was four years ago and we still cry about it but not as much now. Danny, I believe, is free now of mourning for Alice and Jess. He's a very decent, moral, communicative together man. I identify with him when he says that although he has only been acquainted with you for part of a weekend, there's something about you and Jan that he can't explain. And I got that feeling shortly after you had arrived. As near as I can infer, it must be that both spouses died in a car accident.

You know Cindy. I feel that Danny is attracted to me. And I to him and Jan adored him at the outset. I feel that strange pull as well but don't have a clue. But what you said about spouses killed in a car accident seems to resonate with me as well.

Go slow with each other as I know that you both will; you're both sensible.

I like you Cindy. Your open and easy to talk with. I hope that Danny and I can work something out. We'll talk more before we leave. Danny and I need to talk after Jan goes to bed.

Mommy, Danny really helped me with the math. The poem was fun. From now on I will try to learn about the author before I read their work. It really helps if you know the author.

You like Danny, don't you dear?

(Jan smiles and nods her head) Will he be my daddy one day?

It's too early to say, dear. The only thing that I can tell you is that we like each other and that's a good start. And Cindy is very open, honest and nice. I like her.

I like her too. But mommy, if Danny becomes my daddy and your husband, where will we live? Will he live with us or will we live with him?

Those are very good questions, dear and I have no answer for that. Although it's premature now, these are issues that the three of us will have to decide if and when it's necessary. I know that you like Danny and Danny likes you but we've only known each other for about two days.

You're right mommy but I like Danny very much. It seems like I've known him much longer.

Let's talk more about it tomorrow. Get a good night sleep. Pleasant dreams, sweety.

That's what Danny calls me mommy.

Oh! Sleep well dear. (Kisses and covers Jan with a blanket) I'll be back later. Do you want the door open or closed?

Closed please, mommy. (Miriam closes the door gently and joins Cindy, Tagg and Danny on the porch).

Grab a seat, Miriam, saidTagg.

Thank you Tagg. It's a beautiful spring night. The air is fresh and what are those little birds—sounds like thousands of them—in a choir.

They're spring peepers, answered Danny. Like a pandean chorus. They're small tree frogs and they serenade us for weeks. Often, there is no need to talk but to listen to them and deal with your own thoughts.

Thanks for explaining Danny. How peaceful it is up here.

It is, Miriam.

If you'll excuse Tagg and I, we've had a long day.

(Danny hugs Cindy and Tagg). Good night guys.

Goodnight Miriam.

(No talking for a few minutes). Cindy told me that she's pregnant and I'm so happy for them. They decided to have a child after all these years. I'll be an uncle! Tagg is my closest friend who along with Cindy helped me pull through the toughest period of my life. Miriam, after Geoff died, were there people in your life who helped you?

None really, Danny. No, come to think of it, one person. My therapist. Geoff managed to annoy everyone who could have become our friend. My mother and her husband/partner—don't know which— lived on the west coast and she couldn't afford to stay long after the funeral. Oh yes after the funeral! How well I remember. No money, debts, no friends, a young daughter and not knowing what to do. If it weren't for Jan I would have taken an overdose of sleeping pills. I was so lonely for human contact that I would have appreciated a wrong number telephone call. They say that when one door closes, another opens. My next door neighbor is a clinical psychologist and she visited me the following night. We talked for hours. Actually I talked, cried and she listened. She agreed to take me on gratis. It took many months of counseling during which time she managed to get me a nursing job at her hospital. This meant back to the books and courses to upgrade my skills—I was an operating room nurse before Jan was born so fortunately I didn't need a major upgrade of my skills. That's basically it, Danny.

Hmmm. If it weren't for Jan you would have ended it. (said thoughtfully)

Yes!

Strange. As I was going to blow out my brains.....my daughter came to me in a vision which stopped me as I was squeezing the trigger. Alice was with her. I think that I mentioned this on that TV show. Our daughters are the reason we're alive today, Miriam.

You're right, Danny. Danny, I sense that you're a very decent man and Jan adores you. We both have a sensing that we can't figure out that somehow connects us. Do you want to give it a shot to see if we can develop a relationship? And I don't mean hopping into bed to inaugurate the understanding.

Miriam, I would like that. How do you suggest that we go about it?

Let's alternate weekends staying with each other. We both have guest rooms. Danny, I haven't seen your home, come to think of it.

Miriam, it's kinda messy. I'll take you and Jan over tomorrow after breakfast.

Goodnight Miriam, see you and Jan in the AM. No blintzes though.

(Miriam initiates a hug. Danny's knees buckle somewhat and Miriam senses it).

CHAPTER 29

Did you have a good sleep dear.

I dreamed that you and Danny got married.

My goodness, you sure are rushing things. Danny and I had a good talk last night. We both agree that an adult man and woman should get to know each other very well before they get married so here's what we decided: we'll spend weekends with each other getting to know each other. This includes you, dear. Next week, Danny will stay in our guest room, then we will stay in Danny's house which I understand is messy.

Mommy, I'm so excited!

I know dear but it might not work out.

If it doesn't will Danny still be my friend?

You'll have to speak to Danny about it. I hope that he will. Knowing Danny, he would.

I will mommy.

(Cindy knocks on door) May I come in?

Come in Cindy.

Hi Miriam, Jan. You all look very rested. Looks like you both had a good sleep.

We did, Cindy.

Tagg and I will be serving breakfast whenever you're ready. (laughing) Danny's been up since sunrise cleaning his place. He'll be joining us in about 10 minutes.

See mommy. If he didn't love us why would he be up since sunrise cleaning his home for us?

(Cindy laughs).

Jan dear, love takes time between people. I wonder how bad it was before he cleaned it?

Let's say that it wasn't housewife neat, laughed Cindy. Listen to your mommy Jan. I know that you want Danny to be your daddy but be patient. Danny and your mommy have to get to know each other much better which will take time— spending time with each other and with you too. There are things that the three of you will have to resolve. Anyway, I'll leave you two to get dressed and I'll call Danny when you arrive. (laughing). He's finally found the motivation.

Hi Miriam and Jan. Please take a seat in the living room. I'll call Danny. (Tagg calls on the telephone. Whispers. Times up for cleaning Danny boy, Miriam and Jan are here all wearing hungry faces. Five minutes? Okay).

(Danny enters looking like a man who's been cleaning his home furiously). Hi Miriam, hi Jan.

Hi Danny, said Miriam and Jan in unison.

Can I give you both a hug?

Miriam nods and Danny hugs them).

Sorry that I look kind of messy. Had a few odds and ends to look after at the house.

Like what Danny?, joked Miriam.

(Danny picking up the humour). Oh the usual. Miriam, I'm really reasonably neat for a guy, but I've let matters slide the last few months—badly. You and Jan would have walked in, out, and perhaps driven back to the city—bye bye Danny, nice knowing you. Call me next month, year when the wreckage is removed from the hall entrance.

That bad?

(Danny nods and sits facing Miriam). Sort of. Would you and Jan like to take a walk after breakfast if you're not stuffed? Let me show you the property, the gardens, the wilderness.

I'd love to Danny, Jan?

So would I mommy, but Cindy said that she wants me to show her some of my dance routines. She's an instructor. Is that okay mommy?

Miriam, we didn't agree on a specific time, clarified Cindy. (Clarified to make it clear that they're not forcing Miriam to be alone with Danny.

(Danny picking it up as well) After breakfast and clean up, why don't we all go to the studio? After Jan and Cindy shower and change, let's all walk the property.

(Miriam sensing it as well and appreciating Danny's thoughtfulness) Danny, plan A would work for me. Jan can go with Cindy and you can show me around. Are you comfortable with that, Jan? Danny?

Oh yes mommy!

Danny shyly, awkwardly scratches his head. I'm okay too if you are Miriam.

I am Danny.

(After breakfast). Jan dear, have a good session with Cindy.

I will mommy and don't forget to kiss Danny.

Jan! said an embarrassed Miriam noting Danny's red face. You shouldn't….

Miriam, don't be annoyed, said Danny. (As an aside). Jan is understandably anxious, offered Danny.

A little too much.

Let's get on the golf cart. Do you want to drive and me to navigate?

Why not? Thanks for asking.

Hang a right to the Japanese gardens.

(Sitting in the cart) Danny, it's absolutely exquisite. Who designed this?

Mom did the initial project then when Cindy and I

bought out our parents and they slowed their involvement, we added to it. You'll meet my folks later today—they're back from an European trip and are just recovering from jet-lag.

What are they like?

They're gentle, decent, very affectionate with us as with themselves. Fun-loving! Dad was an English major but didn't to into the master and doctoral program as his mother was ill. He worked as a fireman then became assistant fire chief when he met mom. Their 10 day courtship was a blast. Cindy and I consider ourselves blessed for having them as parents. They're still very affectionate with each other—even today—and with us even as adults. What were your folks like?

Mom was a math teacher and dad was an architect. I was raised in what you might call a left-brained home. Dad was fun and mom was serious. They held back on affection—not huggy touchy feely people— which was how they were raised and consequently how they raised me which accounts for the reason I married Geoff. Realized all that in therapy with my neighbour psychologist. My dad died three years ago and mom lives on the west coast with a man whom I haven't met yet.

Miriam, if it weren't for the therapy, the support of friends, I wouldn't be here. I consider that period in my life both the worst period of my life yet an enormous growth period as well, as I had to look and keep on looking within for strength, guidance and meaning. I'm certain that you went through a similar hell.

(Miriam nodded as she would have cried. Danny noting it quickly changes the subject). Let's drive over to our "ashram". This way.

Your ashram?

It's a sacred place for us. Mom first, then dad later, went there to escape from the madding crowd, to resolve issues both personal and interpersonal. That's when they first hugged and realized that they liked each other before their famous manure fight?

Their manure fight?

(Danny tells the story in about 10 minutes—events before, during, after).

(Miriam started laughing. Becoming more at ease with Danny).

Let's get back to Cindy and Jan.

(Miriam gives Danny a hug). You're a decent, fun guy Danny. I'm starting to feel comfortable with you.

Same here Miriam. I'm also a bit petrified.

Danny. I'm still scared by the prospect of being with another man although that's easing off being with you.

Come to think of it, so am I (returning the hug). Let's drive back—hang a right.

Oh mommy, Cindy had a few new routines that were wonderful. We had a shower and changed just as you were driving back. Did you kiss Danny.

Jan!!

Jan, said Danny, actually we hugged each other—twice. The hug simply means we like each other, are comfortable with each other. We don't want to rush things. Do I get a hug now?

Jan nods shyly and they hug.

Miriam, Jan is a natural and I enjoyed the one on one with her.

Thanks for working out with her.

Come on in the house you two and meet my folks.

How nice, Cindy. I'm anxious to meet them; Danny spoke very highly of them.

Miriam, I'm so happy to meet you exclaimed a heavy-set woman with an expression of pure love. Let me give you a hug. (The hug was powerful, exuded such love that Miriam began to cry—she had never received such a loving hug).

Are you okay dear? asked a concerned Jill.

(Composing herself). I'm okay Jill. Just lost it for a moment.

And you must be Jan. I've heard so much about you. (hugs Jan who absorbs it giving Miriam a pleased look). Wow Jill! You give the best hugs ever, said Jan.

Now it's my turn said a handsome trim man with grey hair. I'm Jack, Danny's dad. Miriam, step forward and receive your hug.(Which was almost as powerful as Jill's but Miriam was composed this time.

Now it's your turn sweety.

Danny calls me sweety.

Now we both can call you sweety. (Gives her a warm hug).

Danny, remember you mentioned the restaurant Cru? Cree? Crudee? something where they insult you. Can we go there?

Jan, you shouldn't ask, said Miriam.

(Danny glances at Miriam who nods. Jack and Jill glance at each other and smile knowingly).

Jan, you're on but remember this; you asked for it sweety.

It's really all in fun isn't it Danny?

It really is.

CHAPTER 30

❀

(Giving Jan the once over) Well look who we have here, Pippi Tornstockings. Mommy forgot to darn your socks, Pippi? Whatever happened to your tight braids? Don't tell me. You traded them in for those shiny braces on your teeth.

(Jan starts to giggle as does Miriam as she glances at Danny who is smiling).

Now let's see who you carried here? Ah yes, you dragged your father Ephraim off of his boat. Hey skipper, how's the S.S. Hoptoad and from which port did you find this floozie?

The hoptoad is in dry dock and the floozie is the ship mascot I'll have you know.

(Miriam smiles)

Yah right! Follow me.

Here. Sit!

(Jan is squealing with delight and anticipation. Danny and Miriam are bracing themselves).

I'm your waiter and here are your menus. Make up your minds fast. I'm busy. We're busy. Look around.

Jan, do you see anything that you like? asked Danny.

Yes Danny, closing her eyes. I'll have a Shirley Temple and a cheese burger with a coke.

A drunk at your age Pippi? Your nose will turn red like Bozo the clown. You'll be setting a bad example for the girls of the world who admire you—a pre-teen drunk. And a cheeseburger? Borrrring!! How unimaginative for Pippi.

But a Shirley Temple has no alcohol, laughed Jan.

(Whispers. I know sweety, I can put rum into it when no one's looking)

(Jan laughs) No thank you just the same.

That's what I'm here for sweety.

Okay and you Miss ship mascot?

Oh! I'll have the fish and chips special.

Dessert?

The New York cheesecake looks absolutely scrumptious.

You're kidding lady? With those hips you'll have to start wearing pleated skirts. I can see already that the stitches on your backside (glancing over) are starting to burst at the seams.

(Miriam suppresses a smile).

I'll have a fruit salad. Thank you for your concern.

That's what I'm here for.

And what's your pleasure, skipper?

Let me see. I'll have your spinach quiche. (Danny remembers what Jack ordered years back and the waiter's response. Braces himself).

(Spoken slowly) I should have known. Popeye, a faygeleh! So tell me Popeye, do you occasionally ask a crew member in the shower room to pick up your bar of soap when you're months at sea?

Sometimes. Captain's prerogative you know. We get desperate as well you know.

(Miriam is laughing behind the menu).

I smell mutiny, Captain Bly says Danny. (waiter leaves)

This place is cool, said a delighted Jan.

Do you like how he insulted you? asked Danny.

(Jan giggled and nodded).

That was really a delicious meal and a fun place Danny. Can we go again soon? asked Jan.

Jan, if we go too soon, it might not be funny anymore. But, we can talk about it and I'm certain that you'll tell your classmates about it.

Thank you for taking us. Those nasty, crusty old men were hilarious. I'll tell the staff at the hospital about Crudité.

It's 2:00PM. Do you want to go back to our farm and rest? Dinner will be ready at 5:00PM.

Danny, can we go to the dump to watch the bears? I've never seen bears in the wild, asked Jan.

(Danny looks at Miriam who nods).

Sure! let's go.

(Whispering) Miriam, I hope that you didn't mind me deflecting the various decisions regarding Jan at you as you're her mother.

I appreciate that Danny.

Here we are at the dump. Hey Jeff, where are the bears today?

There are six of them at the garbage sight—right there.

Miriam, Jan, look at them.

Mommy, they are 50 feet away and feeding on garbage. I thought that they ate berries only.

Sweety, the garbage is very available to them and always in the same place same time and always enough for many bears, said Jeff.

Mommy, everybody calls me sweety up here.

That's because you are a sweety, smiled Jeff.

Jeff, my two friends from the city: Miriam and her daughter Jan.

Pleased to meet you and whenever you're feeling in the dumps, please drop in on me.

Thank you Jeff, we'll consider it, said Miriam with a smile.

Jan and Miriam, face the bears. I'll get the digi-camera out of my back pack and snap a few, said Danny. Great, now face me and I'll snap you with the bears behind you. Great! Let's view them.

Oh mommy, one bear stopped eating, stood up on his hind legs and was looking at us when we were facing Danny.

I think that the bear wanted to be in the picture, replied Danny.

(Jan giggled).

I'll e-mail them to you tonight so that you could print them when you're back home.

Danny, will you ask Jeff to take a picture of the three of us with the bears in the background?

Be happy to said Jeff who was in earshot. Smile! Got it!

Oh Danny. That's a beautiful picture. I'll print it out when we get home and keep it under my pillow.

Why thank you Jan. Now I think it's time to head back to the farm.

CHAPTER 31

Miriam, dinner will be ready in about half an hour. Why don't you and Jan freshen up. Danny decided to go home to take a shower as he's been up since sunrise and has been busy all day. Oh, here he is.

Hi Miriam hi Jan. Jan runs to Dannny for a hug and holds her cheek out for a kiss.

(Danny hugs and kisses her cheek) Wow Jan! That's some greeting. Hadn't had one like...(catches himself) ... for along time.

Like from Jess? asked Jan. We talked to each other last night.

Jan, asked Miriam, what's all this about? You never mentioned that to me.

What? You talked to Jess? What did she say? asked Danny.

I dreamed that we were doing a routine together then took a break. She asked me to "take care of my daddy. He'll be your daddy one day". "Really" I asked. "Really" she said then disappeared.

Jan, this is somewhat embarrassing. I appreciate your sharing your dream with us. We like each other but it's really too soon as we've only known each other for a few days.

I'm sorry mommy, Danny. It's like I've known Danny for years. Danny if your house is clean, can we sleep in your guest room?

(Again Danny looks at Miriam who shrugs her shoulders this time).

Miriam, Jan, after dinner let's take a drive to my home. I'll show you around then I'll leave you and mommy alone to decide. I'll be happy with whatever your decision because we'll still be together. If not at my place, then at Cindy and Tagg's which is five minutes away.

That sounds fair and reasonable said Miriam. How do you feel about it Jan?

I'm anxious to see Danny's house said an excited Jan.

Miriam, Tagg and I will do the dishes as you have some serious matters to consider.

Miriam, good luck dear said Jill. May I give you a good luck hug before Jack and I retire for the night?

Certainly Jill.

The hug was even more powerful with loving energy than before and Miriam could just barely keep herself composed.

And here is your hug sweety. (Jan felt the loving energy.

I'll skip the hugs tonight said Jack as I even felt those hugs. Good night Miriam, good night sweety.

Good night Jack, Jill said Miriam and Jan in unison.

CHAPTER 32

Danny, I love the pine furniture and lace curtains. It's perfect for the setting. I can't get my eyes off the fireplace. The granite stones with the fire reflecting off the walls gives it a warm, comfortable feeling.

Thanks Miriam. I had to refurnish after Alice died in order not to go mad. Mom and Cindy helped me chose a plan. Then it was a matter of checking auctions, estate sales especially where older folks were selling off before going into retirement or nursing homes. There's quite a selection available in the area. I had the fireplace put in as I needed time to read, think, meditate, cry in a sacred place of my own. (Changing the subject). Jan, did I clean my home well enough for you and mommy?

Danny! You have an exercise room here—for dancers. Mirrors are on all the walls.

Alice taught dance classes here as well. Her music studio was in the next room.

Danny, may I warm up and stretch at the bars?

(Glancing quickly at Miriam who nods). Go for it, Jan. (Jan gets a feel for the bars and the room).

Let's look at the guest room. My bedroom is in here. (Door was closed).

Oh Danny, may I see your bedroom?

(Glancing quickly at Miriam who shrugs)

Jan, I know that you want to see where I sleep and dream

but let's look at it later. I want to show you and mommy first to your room.

(Opens the door). Oh Danny, it's a king-sized four poster with lots of pillows, exclaimed Jan.

So you and mommy could have a pillow fight before you go to bed. Off the bedroom is the bathroom. Come over and I'll show you how the Jacuzzi and sauna work. You girls might like a sauna and steam before bedtime—you'll sleep like babies. (Shows them the controls and demonstrates). The towels are here in abundance. It's getting late. If you need anything simply knock on my door anytime. Good night girls.

Mommy! Lying on the bed is like floating on a cloud.

Isn't it! Let's get ready for bed. You go first. Shower, then if you like, go into the Jacuzzi—it'll give you a gentle massage. I'll shower after you, I'll skip the Jacuzzi then we can sit in the sauna together, then shower together—we can scrub each others back—then to a comfy bed.

Sounds fantastic mommy.

(In bed together) Mommy, I never saw daddy gave you a hug. Jill gave me a hug that was so loving. Everyone hugs everyone here. Mommy are you listening?

Oh, I'm sorry, dear. I'm sorry. My thoughts were elsewhere. I never received a hug like Jill's. I felt a rush of loving energy shoot through me. It made me rethink part of my life which came to me in a flash: I had never realized it but from childhood on I was starved for the loving touch of another human being. My parents were not touchy, feely, huggy people. This is a touching, feeling, hugging loving family. When Jill first hugged me I started to cry (starts to cry) because I was reminded in a flash what I've been starved for all these years.

You see mommy. It's what I've been trying to tell you. Danny will be a good huggy husband for you and a huggy daddy for me.

You're impossible, dear. But maybe you're right. (Composing herself)

That was a lot of fun, Jan. We've never showered together.

I don't remember you ever scrubbing my back mommy.

(Both shed tears for a moment). Good night Jan. (Miriam kisses Jan, covers her with the duvet then gets into bed.

(Miriam is restless and finally falls asleep but wakes up around 2:00AM. Gets out of bed, walks down the hall, enters Danny's room and lies down beside Danny who wakes).

Miriam, what's wrong? asked Danny half wake.

Danny please hug me... hug me, hold me, nothing more.

What? (Waking). I'd love to Miriam.

(Both in foetal position facing each other, Danny places his arm lovingly around Miriam but making certain that all she feels is his arm and body. They lay like that for a while then Miriam opens up). Danny, Jill reminded me what I have been starved for all my life. Geoff was sparing of affection but he did hug me the night before he died and it felt so good. I'll never forget the events of the following morning four years ago: June 5th at 10:05. Actually it wasn't too far from here.

What! said a shocked Danny. June 5th at 10:05 AM? Was Geoff driving a black SUV?—I forget the model.

Why yes, he was...oh my god. No!

The wetness they shared were their respective tears.

Come on Jess, our work here is finished. Danny dearest, we'll always be in your heart but it will never interfere in the loving relationship that you will develop with Miriam. Goodbye my love.

And daddy, you'll be a good daddy for Jan. I love you.

(Miriam woke first at sunrise as the morning light was peeking through the curtains and studied Danny's face. There was a peacefulness, lightness that she had never seen before. She observed his muscular torso which was uncovered by the sheets. Danny opened his eyes slowly and was aware of Miriam staring at him. He was lying on his side facing Miriam lying on her side facing him. He noticed a radiance in Miriam that he hadn't noticed before. Rolling onto his back to stretch his arms and legs then returning on his side where he noticed her very feminine figure).

Miriam dear, my daddy wrote many years ago that male hormones are strongest in the morning.

Really! said Miriam as she gently pushed Danny down onto his back. Why don't you— easing herself slowly on top of him, caressing his face with her gently-scented shoulder-length hair and sliding her boobs slowly across his chest— tell me all about it?

THE END

Epilogue

Danny, Miriam, Jan.

Danny and Miriam married after a short courtship and set up home on the farm. Shortly after Miriam and Jan moved, an operating room nurse retired and Miriam was hired. Danny adopted Jan who adored him and she was the apple of his eye becoming very active in her upbringing: tutoring her, taking her to dance classes, art galleries, theatres, museums, teaching her how to fish, spread manure, clean the barn together—with the occasional manure fight—and working the land and farm machinery and sharing his spiritual values. Miriam, it turned out, had an insatiable congenital need for hugs and affection which Danny was happy to provide. Jan who couldn't have asked for a better male role model than Danny, became a veterinarian and set up her practice from the farm. Farmers knew that Jan would barter her services if they lacked the cash or pay whatever they could whenever they could. Money was never Jan's raison d'etre.

Danny and Miriam both retired in the same year to live out their lives on the farm.

Danny never forgot Alice and Jess: in his heart and soul they were always there. Memory of them never ever interfered with his love for Miriam and Jan with whom he had a good life. The human brain has this wonderful facility.

Sally, Kate, Carol, Judy

Despite moving far away with their husbands, they were constantly in touch. Christmas, Thanksgiving, Passover were shared and alternated with their respective families:children, grandchildren, boy friends, girl friends. They were truly friends for life.

Beatrice and Allan.

They had a wonderful life together. Allan died peacefully in his sleep at age 52. Beatrice died two months later of a broken heart mourning Allan's passing every waking hour.

Jack place the following inscription on their memorial stone: They loved each other A bushel and A peck.

Cindy and Tagg

(Cindy and Miriam grew to be like sisters to each, inseparable, sharing everything. Danny and Tagg couldn't have been any closer. They sold the business to Tagg junior who was a brilliant landscape architect and a decent human being. They too retired to the farm to live the remainder of their lives along with Danny and Miriam where they would occasionally reminisce about their childhood and how blessed they were to have Jack and Jill as parents. Miriam, Jan and Tagg junior ate this all up and loved to hear the stories).

Jack and Jill.

(Danny, Miriam, Jan, Cindy, Tagg and Tagg junior made a surprise 50th wedding anniversary for Jack and Jill).

Surprise! Happy 50th anniversary mom and dad as they enter the Redneck Review.

(Jack and Jill were stunned momentarily. Then have tears).

(Jill composing herself first and viewing Cindy, Danny, Tagg, Tag junior, Danny, Miriam and Jan). Why thank you kids. You've planned this and managed to keep it a secret. We're impressed, grateful that we can all be here said Jill.

(Jack, composed). I'll say.

Mom and dad. We want you dance to your favorite song, said Cindy and Danny in unison.

(Jack and Jill look lovingly at each other. Jack takes Jill by the hand, places his arm around Jill, waits for the music, and then they dance. Each are in their thoughts began reviewing their lives together which they felt was blessed despite Alice's and Jessica's death).

(I can't remember when you weren't there
When I didn't care for anyone but you
I swear we've been through everything there is
Can't imagine anything we've missed
Can't imagine anything the two of us can't do

Hey Jill, you will never believe this. I just had a fire in the kitchen this morning which was put out very quickly after the fire trucks arrived. When the assistant fire chief came over to make certain that I was okay, which I was thanks to their fast response, I noticed that he had no ring on his finger. Knowing that he must be busy, I had to work quickly.

Hi Jill, you don't know me. My name is Jack and your friend Joan gave me your telephone number.

Oh, you're the fireman. Oh, I shouldn't have said that thought Jill.

Why yes! I earn my living as a fireman.

. Don't give her the obvious once over. She'll see it. Look her in her face, in her eyes. Open your heart to her. Determine the quality of who the person really is that resides in her body.

If he gives me the once over and stops at my ass and grimaces like most of them, it will be a short date. But, on the other hand, give him a chance. Guys are guys and they all seem to want these slim string bikini types with big boobs.

Through the years, you've never let me down
You turned my life around, the sweetest days I've found
I've found with you ... through the years
I've never been afraid; I've loved the life we've made
And I'm so glad I've stayed, right here with you
Through the years

If you find that you've gained ten pounds or so, please consider coming to me and crying about it —I'll love it. I will tell you to gain 10 more pounds, that it wont make any difference to me, that there's more to grab, that women have to be fat— in the right places of course. I'll mean it.

BINGO!

Hey Jill, look at this. Catch this horseball.

I can't remember what I used to do
Who I trusted whom, I listened to before
I swear youve taught me everything I know
Can't imagine needing someone so
But through the years it seems to me
I need you more and more

...would you like to stay for the night?

Yes and no. Yes! I'm quite attracted to you and you know it. Under other circumstances I would have gladly said yes and I've been there before. No because I need and want to know you better, that what we feel for each other is genuine and not as a result of a turn on. You're a gem and I don't want to mess things up. I know that you're not a loose woman and you're just as much turned on to me as I to you. Intimacy will draw me closer to you and want to know and feel that it would be reciprocated. I don't want to suppress my emotions during intimacy. If I love you I will tell you that not only during periods of intimacy but at other times as well. Also, not while were both smelling and covered with manure and we don't know each other well enough to shower together.

Through the years, through all the good and bad
I knew how much we had, I've always been so glad
To be with you ... through the years
It's better everyday, you've kissed my tears away
As long as its okay, I'll stay with you

Through the years

Jill, I'm really falling in love with you. I'm so tired. I'm rolling over, good night. Sorry!

Isn't that always the way with you guys. I'll open the window and waft away your effluvium with a towel. Now let me fall asleep with my arm around this gorgeous hunk.

Key of "G" —George
As I hold you close tonight
Hear what I say
There's no doubt it's love alright
'Cause I never felt this way
An angel's what you are
And now I see
You're not just some one else
You're something special to me

So you enjoyed my love song to you. Why don't you tell me about it? I'll pull off the highway and park over there in that secluded area where you can really tell me—— all about it. Here, in the back seat where my hearing is more acute.

Jack, where are you taking me? Jack, whatever are you doing?,

Can't think of an answer, honey, every last drop of my blood is concentrated in my nether regions. There's none left for my brain.

You're an animal Jack.

Through the years, when everything went wrong

257

Together we were strong, I know that I belonged
Right here with you ... through the years
I never had a doubt, we'd always work things out
I've learned what loves about, by loving you
Through the years
Yo!, I'll try.

Jack, sweetheart, are you nuts?

Ah hon, it's all in good fun.

Hey folks, now here's a brave man. Give him a hand. What your name sonny?

Just call me Jack.

Whuch you gonna dance to?

How about David Rose's The Stripper.

Wake up wake up

What, what's going on?

Jack, your vacation ends today and you haven't discussed your intentions with me, us.

Jill, I've been doing a lot of thinking. It's been a lot of fun and it's difficult for me to have to tell you this........that I quit my job and want to be with you for the remainder of my life.

You bastard!

Amos, I love this woman and want to be with her for the rest of my life and don't want to return. Forget my vacation, holiday pay and any unused pay credits. Please don't ask me to give you adequate notice as that will mean weeks without Jill. She can't leave her business as she's just begun a huge project and I'm helping her.

Through the years, you've never let me down
You've turned my life around, the sweetest days I've found
I've found with you ... through the years
It's better everyday, you've kissed my tears away
As long as it's okay, I'll stay with you
Through the years!

(Still embracing and whispering to each other) I don't know about you, hon, but during the dance, memories of how we met and our courtship came flashing through my head.

Dearest. The same with me.

Let's share which memories those were later tonight— in bed perhaps?

Beast!

(Jack and Jill died the following morning and were found in their bed by Cindy and Danny when they didn't show up for breakfast.

They died embracing each other—Jack had an erection, Jill his semen. They had requested in their wills that they be buried together. And that's exactly how they were buried— in one large coffin embracing each other. Buried inside their hut on the far side of their property with a simple grave marker.

They had always realized how blessed their lives were: soul mates who found each other and still playful and sexually active with each other after 50 years of marriage including to the day of their death; their children and their families living together harmoniously and supporting each other on the farm— how families lived traditionally in a foregone era).

Life brings its joys and tragedies and despite the latter, they all made a good life.

Crudite'

But before I leave you, dear readers, Crudite' became a very successful, affordable franchise giving employment to legions of crabby, crusty old men, women and retired stand-ups; where to be insulted, humiliated and to be mocked was *plat de jour.*